Rough Justice

M. A. COMLEY

ISBN-13:978-1507854808

ISBN-10:1507854803

Rough Justice

New York Times bestselling author M A Comley

Published by M A Comley

Copyright © 2014 M A Comley

Digital Edition, License Notes

OTHER BOOKS BY

M A COMLEY

Blind Justice

Cruel Justice

Impeding Justice

Final Justice

Foul Justice

Guaranteed Justice

Ultimate Justice

Virtual Justice

Hostile Justice

Tortured Justice

Rough Justice

Forever Watching You

Evil In Disguise – Based on True events novel.

Deadly Act (Hero series novella) coming Feb 2015

Torn Apart (Hero Series #1)

End Result (Hero Series #2)

Sole Intention (Intention Series #1)

Grave Intention (Intention Series #2)

Keep in touch with the author at
http://www.facebook.com/pages/Mel-Comley/264745836884860
http://melcomley.blogspot.com
http://melcomleyromances.blogspot.com
Subscribe to newsletter

R.I.P. my darling Henry. I hope your journey to the Rainbow Bridge was a successful one. Thank you for the 14 years of devotion, no dog will ever replace you. You'll live on in my heart and in the pages of the Justice books. Please continue to watch over us.

You are my guiding light, beam brightly forever more my precious friend.

This book is dedicated to a special vet, Frantz Marin, for the compassion he showed while caring for my beloved dogs, Sammy and Henry during 2012 and 2014.

This book is also dedicated to my beautiful Mum, Jean, for her never-ending support.

Special thanks to my wonderful editor Stefanie and Joseph for proofreading.

And finally, my eternal thanks, go to Karri Klawiter for the wonderful cover as always, you're a very talented lady.

ROUGH JUSTICE

Prologue

Feeling the constant need to shudder, Noelle walked through the deserted streets. She wasn't sure if the sensation was due to the slight chill in the air or the events that had occurred earlier that evening while she was at work. A noise sounded behind her, and a sharp glance over her shoulder to see if anyone was following her caused pain to rip through her neck.

"Damn, that bloody hurt!"

The alley was empty, no trace of a stalker in sight. She pulled her fake-fur coat around her scantily-clad body and upped her pace. *Why the bloody hell did I leave the car at home tonight?* Noelle's stint at the club had proved to be an anxious one that evening. Three of the punters had tried their hardest to grope her at different intervals during her routine on stage. Not for the first time, thoughts of paying off her student loan quickly sprung to mind. Once that was paid, she would be able to pack in the crappy job and begin her life in earnest. She dreamed of the day when she could announce to her parents that she had successfully started up her own architect business. They would be mortified if they knew about the sordid secret existence she'd led the last few years. *How else am I supposed to pay off my loan and feed myself?* All she was trying to do was exist. She didn't do drugs, unlike most of the girls who worked with her, but her parents had no idea how expensive the cost of living was for a single person in the London area. So she flaunted the one desirable thing God had gifted her: a slight but perfectly formed body, which the men seemed to enjoy ogling and sneakily touching when she was on stage.

Every girl rehearsed her routine down to the finest detail, and the security team did their utmost to ensure the punters didn't get the opportunity to grope the girls. However, things had kicked off big time in the club that night, and the security boys had been preoccupied with ejecting a rowdy group of Noelle's fellow students, but that had come too late for Noelle. Three of the drunken louts had taken it in turns to pounce on her, groping every bare inch of her flesh—and her skimpy outfit exposed plenty. She shuddered again at the thought of their vile hands pinching and pulling at her skin and her costume, hoping to expose yet more flesh. The night had left a very sour taste in her mouth. Feeling cheap and dirty, she reinforced her determination to get out of the job sooner rather than later.

Another noise caught her attention. Supporting her aching neck with one hand, she glanced over her shoulder only to find the alley was still clear. Maybe her stroll through the area had disturbed a stray animal rummaging for food in the overflowing bins.

She quickened her pace and walked into the lit main street, breathing out a huge sigh of relief when she reached the end of the alley. A few taxis whizzed past, taking the stragglers home from the nightclub. She raised her hand a couple of times, and one of the drivers she used regularly motioned for her to stay where she was and he would return in a few minutes to pick her up. Any other night, she would have waited.

Not tonight, though. Fear of being followed urged her to seek out an alternative ride home. She trotted as fast as she could in her stiletto sandals, to the taxi rank two streets away. She strained her ear, listening for any further movement behind her. Thankfully, she heard nothing.

She opened the rear door of the black cab. "Hey, Don. Boy, am I glad to see you."

"Jump in, Noelle. Rough night, was it?"

"Yeah, you could say that." She scanned the area again before the taxi moved off, and she caught sight of a figure lurking in the shadow. Urgently, she begged the driver, "Get me home, quickly, Don."

"Sure thing, love. Nippy out there tonight." The driver seemed oblivious to Noelle's fright.

The taxi pulled away from the curb, and Noelle kept an eye on the spot where the stranger had retreated. When the car turned the corner at the end of the road, she couldn't make out if the person, who remained obscured in the darkness, was male or female. An icy chill surged through her veins when she realised someone *could* have been stalking her.

Don chatted casually during the course of the short journey, and Noelle was grateful for the distraction. The driver dropped her off at her flat within ten minutes. She handed him the money for the fare, smiled, and warily got out of the taxi.

"Are you all right, sweetheart? Want me to see you to your door?"

Noelle waved away his kind gesture. "I'll be all right. You get off. I'd hate you to keep your customers waiting." During the ride, she'd heard the controller contact him about another job.

"Okay, Noelle. You take care. See you soon." Don pulled away, leaving Noelle scanning the area.

She swiftly made her way into the covered doorway of the flats. Using her key to the outer door, she entered the building and secured the door behind her. The flat she called home was on the ground floor at the rear of the property. She cautiously opened the door and then chastised herself for being so foolish. Whoever had followed her through the alley had stayed there. She knew no one ever got into the building uninvited, but that thought did very little to push aside her fears. She switched on every light in the flat and filled the kettle to make a cup of cocoa to help settle her nerves. Walking into the bedroom, she tore off her tiny outfit and stepped into her leopard-print fleecy onesie, which always comforted her and helped to block out the seedy part of her life.

Back in the kitchen cum lounge, she poured her drink. Then she returned to the bedroom, where she hopped into bed and picked up her book. Normally, she made herself a cheese sandwich to replenish the calories she burned during her act, but her stomach was churned into too many knots to even contemplate eating. *Nope, I'll settle on having a cocoa then try and sleep.* Noelle had a free morning, but the class she was due to attend after lunch was super challenging. So she needed a good night's sleep to cope with the bombardment of information she knew her lecturer had lined up for the following day. Mr. Crispen was a task master who expected his students to work extra hard. He was from the old school of teaching, the total opposite to some of the younger lecturers, who regularly let their pupils run amok in their lessons.

The warm cocoa calmed her considerably, and before long, she'd headed for the land of Nod. Her dreams turned out to be scarier than what had presented itself that evening, and she sat bolt upright at five a.m., sweat pouring from every inch of her body. "You're being ridiculous. It was just a dream. Go back to sleep."

However, no amount of talking to herself reassured her enough to fall asleep again. She got up and decided to go for a run instead. She hadn't found the time to slot in any form of exercise in more than a month. After slipping on her Lycra jogging pants and a T-shirt, she filled her plastic water bottle from the tap. She left the flat, thankful that the sun was just coming up over the horizon. The park close to her home was a joggers' paradise. There weren't many left in the surrounding area due to the local council closing them down in order to erect yet more flats for the needy or to ease the housing waiting list. She passed a young couple who were regulars at the park and smiled at them. To her surprise, the park was fairly quiet. Noelle reminded herself that not everyone started the day at the crack of dawn.

Jogging round the corner, she saw a group of Chinese people just setting out their exercise mats for their morning Tai Chi class. That was one form of relaxation she was truly desperate to try, and she intended signing up to a class after her term at uni had finished. Although sometimes, the thought crossed her mind that it would be better to join the class right away to combat her anxieties while they were at their peak. She had the instructor's card and made a mental note to ring Mr. Chan later in the day. He waved as she jogged past the group. "Morning. I promise to ring soon." She held her hand up to her ear and extended her thumb and little finger.

He nodded and acknowledged her with a bow.

Noelle could feel her heart rate increasing and the blood pumping through her veins during her exertion as she climbed the slight incline in the park. Off to her left, she saw a middle-aged woman playing fetch with her black Labrador, and a sudden pang of jealousy pricked her skin. She missed her beautiful Missy, the Rottweiler cross she had grown up with. Missy still lived with her Mum and Dad. *I'll ring them later to arrange a visit. It's been a few weeks since I've seen them all.*

Close by, amongst the bushes, she heard a rustling noise. She decided to err on the side of caution and upped her speed. She heard nothing else from that direction. *Is this how it's going to be now?* Because of that one experience, would she obsess over the slightest noise and movement she detected? *Can I really exist like that day in and day out?* No, was the simple answer.

Maybe the next time something occurred, she should have the courage to confront the person outright. Given her current career and the shenanigans she put up with, she knew exactly what the stalker's answer would be. He would leave her alone once she slept with him. Well, there was little chance of that happening. She was off men altogether for the moment. Danny, her last boyfriend, had turned her off men, for the foreseeable future at least. She was enjoying her freedom. Noelle wasn't one of those girls who doubted how good she looked. She'd always felt comfortable in her own skin, and maybe that was why she had become a pole dancer. Apart from her latest mishap, she knew that her work environment was safer than some of the other clubs in the London area. The Tickle Club had a strong reputation of looking after its employees.

Noelle completed another circuit of the park then headed home. The sun's rays were increasing in temperature, and she had the sense to call it a day before the May heat began in earnest. The forecasters had correctly predicted the latest weather front for once. She wasn't usually able to get out for an impromptu run without getting soaked at this time of year.

In the shower, she let the water soak through to her aching legs then soaped her skin. After five more minutes, she reluctantly stepped out and wrapped the soft bath towel around her invigorated body.

Noelle walked back into the bedroom and immediately clutched the towel to her chest. "Who… what… do you want?"

The masked intruder ran his eyes the length of her trembling body before he uttered one whispered word. "You."

Noelle tried to retreat into the bathroom, but her feet remained firmly rooted to the spot. *Shit! What do I do now? Scream? Would the neighbours come to my rescue?* "Please, I have nothing. What little money I have, you can take—"

"Shut up, bitch. I don't want your money. I want *you*." His voice remained constant, never escalating beyond a harsh whisper. He lunged at her.

Noelle quickly twisted sideways to avoid his outstretched arms. He tripped over one of her shoes and fell to the floor. Thankfully, her determination transmitted itself to her legs, and they sprang into action. She ran into the lounge before the attacker could get to his feet.

"Help, please help me. Jennifer, Trevor… *help* me!" she cried out to her neighbours above.

The attacker leapt on her, knocking her to the ground. Her towel slipped. He dropped heavily onto her chest and pinned both of her arms with his knees. As he stared at her nakedness, a guttural moan emanated from his throat.

Noelle struggled to break free, turning her head from side to side, but it was pointless in shifting the man. "Please, let me go. Don't do this."

The man raised his clenched fist and connected with her jaw. In her dazed state, she heard someone knocking on the door to the flat. However, the darkness descended before she could call out for further assistance.

Noelle woke up to find numerous people, including her neighbours from above and police officers, in her lounge. A doctor shone a penlight into her eyes. "Stay where you are for a moment. Let yourself come around naturally. You're safe now."

"What happened... the man..." She tried to lever herself up on her elbows, but the doctor pressed her back down onto the rug.

"He's gone. There was no one here when we arrived."

One of the uniformed policemen stood over her, blocking out the light above. "Are you up to telling us what happened, Miss?"

"I think so. He was here... who was he?"

The policeman's thick lips pulled into a tight smile. "That's what we were hoping you'd tell us, Miss. Did you know the attacker?"

Again, she attempted to sit up, only for the doctor to firmly press her back down. "It's too soon. Stay there," the greying doctor ordered.

"No... at least I don't think I know him. He was wearing a mask, a ski mask."

The policeman noted her responses in his notebook. "Did he speak to you?"

Noelle nodded.

"Did he enlighten you as to the purpose of his visit?" He glared at his colleague, who tutted. He rephrased the question. "What I meant to say was, did he say what he wanted?"

"Me. I told him he could have the small amount of money I have in my purse, but he said all he wanted was me. I tried to get away from him and screamed for help." She scanned the faces and settled on her neighbours. "Thank God you guys were in. Did you hear me?"

Jennifer crouched beside her. "We heard you and called the police right away, sweetheart."

"Did you see him, Jen?"

Jennifer shook her head. "Sorry, no. I'm so glad you're safe."

With her head clearing a little, Noelle tried again to sit upright. This time, the doctor assisted her. "I'm not safe. What if he comes back? He got in here once. What's to say he wouldn't get in again?"

Jennifer looked at one of the officers. "How did he get in?"

"Through a window in the kitchen, we're presuming."

"Has he left any prints on the window?" Jennifer asked him.

Noelle was glad to have Jennifer around. She was a lawyer at a small nearby firm. Noelle wouldn't have had a clue what to ask the police.

"We've placed the call for the Scenes of Crimes department to drop by ASAP. Providing the suspect has left any prints, and those prints are on record…"

Noelle panicked when she saw Jennifer's mouth twist. "What's wrong?"

Jennifer let out a long sigh. "If he wore a mask, the odds aren't good. Did you notice if he was wearing gloves?"

"Everything happened so fast. I was too concerned about covering myself up to notice what was on his hands."

"Think, Noelle. Did he touch you? Close your eyes, imagine him touching you. Were his hands rough or smooth? Covered in fabric or bare?"

Noelle squeezed her eyes closed. At first, all she saw was the outline of the man. In her mind's eye, her gaze dropped to his hands. Disheartened by the image, she informed those gathered around her: "He wore gloves. Damn, there's no hope of catching him now, is there?"

Jennifer rubbed her upper arm. "Don't give up just yet. Let the SOCO team examine the place first, okay?"

"I can't stay here, Jen."

"I can understand that. Can you stay at your parents' house for a few days?"

"No, my parents are on holiday. I suppose I can ring a friend from uni and ask if she can put me up in the meantime."

"Great idea. I'd offer you our spare room, but I think it's a little too close for comfort. It makes sense for you to get well away from here, just in case he comes back," Jennifer said thoughtfully, nodding.

Her legs wobbled in protest as Jennifer helped her into the bedroom. Stopping just inside, Noelle whispered, "Jen, what if he raped me? How would I know?"

Jennifer flung a compassionate arm around her shoulders. "I don't think he had time, Noelle. Maybe we should get the doc to examine you before he goes?"

"I couldn't."

"If you choose not to, then that question is going to remain unanswered and bug you for the rest of your life."

Noelle conceded her friend was talking good sense. "Would you mind asking the doctor for me?"

Jennifer walked her over to the bed then went back in the lounge to have a word with the doctor. She returned with the doctor a few moments later.

"I think you're doing the right thing, Noelle. I'll be as gentle as I can." He turned to Jennifer. "Do you mind leaving us alone?"

Jennifer nodded, rushed forward to give Noelle a hug, and left the room again.

Another three hours passed before everyone finally left the flat. Noelle surveyed her surroundings with such distaste that her questionable feelings began to scare even her. After hurriedly packing a bag, she rang her friend Abbie to tell her she was leaving and would be with her within half an hour.

Taking one final look around the flat, relieved, yet sad to be leaving her treasured home, she tested the windows several times to confirm they were shut properly. She secured the door then left. Her old reliable brown Ford Capri was parked in the car park at the rear of the building. Noelle quickly glanced over her shoulder to make sure she wasn't being watched, then she jumped in the vehicle and locked the car. At two o'clock in the afternoon, the traffic was far easier to combat than she'd anticipated. Two miles into her journey, she felt a shove from behind. Looking in the rear-view mirror at the vehicle, she gasped. "You!"

Noelle tried to outdrive the menacing car following her, but the flow of traffic hampered her attempt. *Maybe the traffic is worse than I thought.* She turned off the main road, trying to lead the other car away from Abbie's house. The decision proved to be the costliest she would ever make when her car spluttered to a halt. Immediately, she glanced down at the dashboard to see that the petrol gauge read empty. She bashed the heel of her hand against the steering wheel. In her haste to get away from the flat, she'd forgotten all about needing to fill the petrol tank. She glanced over her shoulder to see the wicked smile lighting up her pursuer's face as he opened his car door. A tidal wave of fear rippled through her. Within seconds, the man stood menacingly beside the driver's door, as if expecting her to open it. She looked into his eyes. "Why?"

CHAPTER ONE

Lorne laughed when Tony walked into the kitchen. "You can't wear that!"

Tony glanced down at the black suit he was wearing, and with a frown set in place, he met her gaze again. "Why? What's wrong with it? I want to make a good impression, don't I?"

She shrugged. "If that's your intention, then fine. You look more like a funeral director than a bloody PI to me, though."

"Crap, really?"

Lorne crossed the room, linked her arms around the back of his neck, and kissed him. "A dashing, *sexy* funeral director—that's one good thing in your favour."

"Funny. Thanks for the vote of confidence, Mrs. Warner. What do you think I should wear then?"

"Dress casual. No one expects a private investigator to turn up in a whistle and flute. What time are you due to meet Joe?"

Tony looked up at the clock on the wall and ducked out of her arms. "Shit! About ten minutes from now. I haven't got time to change."

"You put your shoes on while I sort out a solution." She went to the laundry basket tucked away in its hiding place under the stairs. At the bottom of the heap, she found his casual brown pullover. She walked back into the kitchen and placed the garment on the kitchen table, where she smoothed out a few of the creases with her hands. "This should do. Slip your jacket off, keep the trousers on. Add this to your ensemble, and that's you looking smart but casual, sort of."

Tony tied the final lace on his shoes, adjusted the strap on his prosthetic leg, and pulled on the sweater. Smiling, he grabbed Lorne, planted another kiss on her lips then bolted for the door. "See you later. Have a good day, hon."

She followed him to the door and waved him off before she went in search of her daughter, Charlie, who was hard at work in the kennels.

"Charlie, are you in here?"

"At the back, Mum." Her daughter's voice drifted the length of the kennel run. Lorne could tell Charlie was still upset.

She opened the kennel door to find Charlie sitting on the foam bed, petting the hairy German shepherd named Sheba. "Is she still a bit down in the dumps?"

"Yeah. Poor girl won't eat her breakfast."

A few days before, Sheba had turned up at the rescue centre, which Charlie and Lorne's friend Carol now ran. Sheba's owner had lost her fight against cancer and had no living relatives to care for the dog. Lorne had a feeling that Charlie was getting very close to the dog and knew the inevitable question would soon leave her daughter's lips. Glancing at the sorrowful-looking dog, Lorne's heart lurched, and in that instant, she knew she would have a hard time turning Charlie down over this particular dog. Maybe the time had come to introduce another furry friend into the household to keep their Border collie, Henry, company while the rest of them were out at work.

"She's had a huge upheaval over the last few days, sweetie. I'm sure she'll come around eventually." Lorne stood behind Charlie and ruffled her hair.

"She'd do far better if she wasn't cooped up in here all day."

Brace yourself. Here comes that killer question! Lorne remained silent.

Charlie tilted her head back and smiled broadly. "Mum... don't you think Henry would love a playmate?"

"He's got lots of playmates right here."

"You know what I mean, Mum. Stop being so awkward. I promise to look after her myself."

"I have no doubts about that. You do a fabulous job caring for all the dogs here. No one is denying that side of things. My main concern is for Henry. He isn't getting any younger. Maybe we should take a step back and consider him in all this. Have you thought about the possibility of his nose getting pushed out if we introduce another dog into the household? Henry loves being the centre of our little world, doesn't he?"

"Yeah, but you've seen him playing with the other dogs. It'll help to keep him young, Mum. Go on, please?"

Lorne closed her eyes, blocking out both her daughter's pleading face and the sadness emanating from Sheba's eyes. They flickered open again when she heard another voice in the kennel. *Saved by the interruption.* "We're in here, Carol."

Carol appeared at the meshed door, a beaming smile sitting happily on her face. "Good morning, both. What a fantabulous day we're having."

"We are?" Lorne asked, amused by her good friend's brightness.

"Oh, yes. The sun is out, the sky is blue, I'm in love, and so are you!"

Lorne burst out laughing, and tears filled her eyes. "When did you add corny poetry to your repertoire?"

"Oh yes, silly me. I'm a poet, and I don't know it. Oh my, there I go again." Her smile quickly vanished when she spotted Sheba's demeanour. "How insensitive of me. Still not doing well, poppet? You know what you need? You need a loving forever home, and I know just the place."

Lorne caught the look between her daughter and her psychic friend and clicked her fingers. "Nice try, you guys. If you think ganging up together and beating me into submission is going to work, think again." Two cheeky grins greeted her, and even Sheba got in on the act when she lifted her head and their gazes locked. Lorne waved a dismissive hand. "I give up. I'm off to work. Have fun, you three."

Charlie's whining, pleading with her to reconsider, followed her out of the kennel and through the main door. She continued to shake her head as she got in the car and headed into London towards the station she called her second home.

DI Katy Foster and constable Alan Jackson, whom everyone called AJ, were studying a graph on the computer screen when Lorne arrived in the incident room. "Morning, you two."

"Morning, Lorne. We're just going over the latest case statistics," Katy said.

Lorne frowned. "Any reason why?"

"Something the super hinted at, really. AJ and I are thinking we might get a directive from head office about the number of cold cases we've accrued over the past year or so."

"Hmm… they don't usually highlight cold cases specifically, do they? Why now?"

Katy perched her bottom on the edge of AJ's desk and folded her arms. "Who knows? Maybe there's been a change at the top. I'd need to look into that. I haven't been made aware of any significant changes lately. Anyway, the super has called a meeting for nine thirty. AJ and I were just trying to get armed with the facts and figures in case she comes down hard on this particular team. Not that we've really had many cold cases over the past couple of years. Maybe some new evidence has come to light on one of our old cases."

"Yeah, that's a more likely reason as to why she's called the meeting. Do you want me to do anything?"

"Nope, just the usual. Check if any cases need our attention from the nightshift. If not, it's paperwork, dreaded paperwork, until then. Hey, how's Tony feeling today?"

"A bit nervous. Not sure how he and Joe are going to find customers to sustain the business and, more to the point, their salaries, but apart from that, he seemed okay when he left this morning."

"He'll do well, I'm sure. He's got an insider on the force, too. That's always a help, right?"

Lorne tilted her head. "Really, you think I'd dish out information willy-nilly like that?" She covered her chest with her hand.

"Don't give me those puppy-dog eyes. We all know what you'll get up to if hubby comes a calling."

"Not me, boss. Let me rephrase that. I wouldn't go behind your back anyway. I'd make sure you gave me the go-ahead first." She smiled broadly.

"Yeah, like I'm going to turn you down. What's his first job? Any idea?"

"Looks like a domestic. The husband wants to know what his wife is getting up to while she's working ten-hour shifts at work."

"Does she work?" Katy asked.

"Apparently, she's a social worker."

"Really? And he's doubting her because?" Katy frowned.

"Not sure if he has a case or not. He seems to think she doesn't spend all her time at work for some reason. Hey, as long as he pays for Tony and Joe's time, then who are we to question the ins and outs of a person's suspicious mind?"

Katy shrugged. "I just don't get some people. Maybe he should consider putting her on a leash to ease his suspicions." Katy shot AJ a warning glance. "Don't you ever get any ideas along those lines, will you?"

AJ's eyes widened. "Wouldn't dream of it."

Katy patted the back of his hand. "I'm sure you wouldn't. It helps that we know where each other is twenty-four-seven, doesn't it?"

"Helps? Is that what you call it?" AJ grumbled unconvincingly, pretending that he felt henpecked.

Katy slapped him gently around the back of the head just as the super and DCI Sean Roberts stepped into the room.

Lorne cringed for Katy, whose cheeks immediately coloured up when she spoke to her two immediate superiors. "Morning, ma'am, sir. Lovely day today."

The super and the chief looked at each other and shook their heads. "I wasn't aware you treated this place as a playground when we're not around, Inspector," Roberts chastised Katy without any hint of a smile.

Katy tried to make excuses for her behaviour, but the super waved away her attempt.

"Gather around, team. The chief and I would like your full attention for this."

The other three members of the team assembled their chairs close to Lorne, Katy, and AJ while Superintendent Anne White and Chief Roberts walked across the room to the incident board. Roberts picked up the marker pen and wrote a name on the whiteboard. He circled it three times.

"Noelle Chesterfield. Does the name ring a bell with anyone?"

Blank looks answered the super's question. Lorne's usually astute mind searched into every crevice but came up with nothing. "Should it?" she asked.

The super glanced at Lorne. "Well, she wasn't one of this team's cases when she went missing. Nevertheless, the file has ended up on my desk, and after briefly looking through it, I think we should take up the woman's case."

"Any particular reason why you've singled out this case, Super?" Katy asked. "I'm taking it that this is one of the cold cases you hinted at earlier."

"That's right. She's sort of a friend of a friend, if you like. I know that head office is being picky about the number of cold cases each department have clocked up in the past year, and this one just happened to be mentioned to me when I attended a party at the weekend."

"A party?" Lorne asked.

"What, Sergeant Warner? Are you surprised that I would attend a party or the fact that such a thing should be brought up as a topic of conversation?"

"Sorry, ma'am. I meant it's strange to talk about such things when you're supposed to be having fun."

The super snorted. "Fun? I've never had fun at any party arranged by the force. Maybe 'party' was the wrong description for the little get-together. One of my closest friends retired from the force last month—Superintendent Colleen Cross. Anyone know her? Anyway, her friend Jennifer attended the party, and I was introduced to her. At first, the woman appeared a little reluctant to make my acquaintance. However, once I unleashed my dazzling personality, she opened up a little. I wasn't expecting her to unveil such a heart-breaking tale, though. A few months back, six months to be exact, one of Jennifer's neighbours and best friends went missing." The super paused as if gauging the team's reaction. "This is the key point that sparked my interest, if you will. The day before Noelle went missing, she'd found an intruder in her flat. He attacked her, and she managed to call out for help. Jennifer, who was in the flat above, realised the gravity of the situation and called the police right away. When the police broke down the door to the flat, they found Noelle Chesterfield lying unconscious on the living room floor. It looked like the intruder had escaped through a window at the back of the flat. No one saw him either enter or leave the property."

"So when exactly did Noelle go missing?" Lorne was the first to ask.

"The woman was understandably terrified by the ordeal and just wanted to get out of the flat as soon as possible. She called a friend and arranged to stay with the friend for a few days until she felt safe enough to return home. The thing is, while en route to the friend's house, Noelle just disappeared."

"How was she travelling to the friend's house? Public transport? Could this be leading up to a coincidental incident?" Katy queried.

"Her own car. That's not the impression I'm getting, Inspector. Maybe that's what the investigating officers on the case thought, too."

Lorne frowned, annoyed that the two incidents hadn't automatically been linked. "Who were the investigating officers?"

"Well, that's the crux of the matter and why I thought we should tackle this case. The two officers dealing with it have since been suspended."

"For what?" Katy asked before Lorne could get the question out.

"They were on the take. You name it, they did it, from forging evidence to beating up suspects and everything in between. I can't really go into specific details at present because of the ongoing investigation into their activities. Let's just say that almost a hundred of their unsolved and solved cases are being scrutinised right now."

Lorne sat forward in her chair. "Shit! Does that mean some of the convictions they achieved are going to be likely overturned? Are they long convictions?"

"They vary considerably. It's a total mess right now and is going to take months to sort out. Each department is going to be asked to re-investigate a mixture of all the cases these two morons had anything to do with. As if we aren't under enough stress to meet targets already, now something as major as this comes our way."

Roberts cleared his throat, ready to speak. "We're used to working under pressure, Super, so I'm sure the team will do all they can to put things right on the cases they're allocated."

"I have every confidence that will be the case, Chief Roberts. I would like this case to be top of the list though, yes?"

"Of course, if that's what you want, Super. We'll get started on it today," Katy said, eyeing Lorne for agreement.

Lorne nodded and took out her notebook to jot down what she'd heard about the case so far.

"Okay, that's great. In total, we have five cases to tackle. I'd like you to work those into your schedule over the next week or so. Let's show the higher-ups what a super-efficient team we are. That is, if they aren't already aware of that snippet of information. I do my best to tout how great you are at every opportunity. Don't let me down on this one, or these cases, right, guys?"

"No, ma'am." The group responded in unison.

"Katy, come back to the office with me to collect the file, will you? Good luck, team. Don't hesitate to call on either the chief or myself if you feel any uncertainty about any of the cases."

The meeting drew to a close, and Katy followed the super out of the incident room. Sean Roberts stayed behind. Lorne issued instructions to the team then approached her boss and good friend. "You look very distant, Sean. Everything all right with the baby?"

"What? Oh yes, she's growing fast. No problems there. What do you make of all this, Lorne?"

"Going over the cases, you mean?"

He nodded.

"Well, I do have some reservations, I must admit. It's never ideal revisiting old cases at the best of times, let alone when they're likely to highlight a detective's negligence."

"That's my thoughts exactly. Yes, the super has confidence in the team to carry out the necessary thorough investigations, but she's also expecting swift results on some really complex cases—as is head office, of course—and some of them go back almost a decade."

"Bloody hell! You mean some folks have been banged up for that long, and they could be totally innocent? Why aren't we being asked to tackle those cases first?"

"The thought had crossed my mind. Other departments are involved in all those cases, so we're having to tread carefully there. Apparently, they've assembled a crack team of officers to work on nothing else but the convictions. Let's hope they can sort out the innocent victims and those who seriously need their convictions to be upheld. Not a task I'd relish, that's for sure. Anyone deemed innocent will be entitled to, and be expecting, compensation, rightly of course. Nevertheless, that compo will need to come from somewhere, and with the department cuts being dished out at present, it doesn't bode well for the future."

"I can understand your concerns, Sean. Shit, we're going to be in the firing line from all sides when this comes out in the press then."

"Yep, you're not wrong there."

"Is that seriously all that's worrying you?" Lorne asked.

"Yes and no. I'll come and cry on your shoulder when I've sorted myself out. It's nothing major, just a few life-changing decisions I need to make over the coming months."

"Oh, that's all right then, if they're only life-changing decisions we're talking about." Lorne smirked then whispered, "I take it some kind of change in job is on the cards?"

"Maybe. Like I said, I'm weighing up my options—our options as a family—right now."

Lorne knew when to refrain from pushing Sean too hard for information. She had a feeling his decisions revolved around a possible move out of the area. He'd been back in London for over five years and had served in the Manchester force, like the super and

Katy, before then. She'd always been under the impression that Sean loved living in the London area. Maybe his wife was behind his indecision. From what Lorne could remember, Carmen Roberts was born and bred up north, not that Lorne had spent much time with Sean's wife since they'd come south, what with what had gone on between Sean and Lorne in the past. Not every spouse appreciated exes working alongside each other. Tony was an exception to the rule—he trusted Lorne implicitly, and she reciprocated that trust. Women were different, though.

She patted her own shoulder and winked at him. "It's always there for you to cry on, at work or at home. You know that, right?"

"I appreciate that, Lorne. Hey, isn't today lift-off day for Tony's new business? Your old business reincarnated, I mean?"

"That's right. He left for work looking like a teenager going off to uni for the first time this morning."

"He's collaborating with another former MI6 officer, isn't he?"

"Yep, Joe Callen and Tony should make a shit-hot team once the right work comes their way. He's chasing up an infidelity case today. I think that kind of work is going to drive him round the twist, I know it would me. That's the main reason I returned to the force really—for much meatier cases to solve."

"I wish them luck anyway. And yes, the day you returned was to our benefit. I can positively vouch for that. You're still okay with the fact that you returned as a sergeant and not an inspector, aren't you?"

"Sometimes I miss not being in charge, but mostly, I'm pleased someone else is in the firing line to take any grief you might dish out when a case gets screwed up."

Sean laughed. "I can totally understand that feeling. I sometimes wish I could hand over the baton to someone else and just sit back and relax for a change. Maybe that'll come to fruition in the next…"

"Go on? Don't stop there, you infuriating…"

"Yes, Sergeant? What derogatory name were you about to call me?" he asked, grinning.

Katy reappeared before they could take their conversation any further. "If you've finished with my sergeant, Chief? I'm under strict instructions to get this case started immediately."

"We were just bidding each other a fond farewell, Inspector. Give me a ring if I can be of any assistance, and good luck. I have a feeling you're going to need it on this one."

Lorne issued the chief with a scornful glance and whispered. "I haven't finished with you, Sean Roberts."

He chuckled and left the incident room as Lorne followed Katy to her office.

Katy threw the file on the desk, removed her jacket, and placed it on the chair behind her. "We've got a week to ten days, tops."

"To solve the case? Jesus, do they expect us to work eighteen hours a day on it?" Lorne sank heavily into her chair.

"Nope, no overtime. They're just expecting us to pull out all the stops and to dig far deeper than these two goons ever did." Katy opened the file and began reading out the case information.

"Is that it?" Lorne asked incredulously.

"Yep. Pathetic doesn't even cover it, does it?"

"Do you think they simply discarded the case in order to sink their teeth into something more profitable? Bearing in mind they were on the take, I'm imagining a lot of backhanders going on, correct?"

"Looks that way." Katy flung herself back in the chair and crossed her arms.

"Okay, I can see how pissed off you are about this, Katy, but that frame of mind is only going to prove detrimental taking this case forward. You and I can do this—I *know* we can."

"I have no doubt about that, Lorne. The problem is it's almost six months since Noelle went missing. What if some kind of lunatic has the girl trussed up in chains somewhere? Granted, she might be dead already or simply run off without letting any of her friends and family know, but I have this terrible image of her being held captive and kept at a vile perpetrator's beck and call, sex wise."

"Then you have to squeeze past that image and think positive about the outcome. If this young woman is still alive, we *will* find her. If on the other hand, she has been killed, then we'll do everything in our power to find her body so her parents can lay her to rest. Her parents are still alive, aren't they?"

Katy nodded and sat forward to study the file again. "Yes, I have their address here. We should visit them first, I guess."

"I would. Maybe we should see if they've called the station on a regular basis first, trying to keep abreast of the case." Lorne reflected on when the Unicorn had kidnapped Charlie years ago and how she'd felt at the time. She didn't sleep and lived on her nerves until she herself had rescued her baby. A scenario like that would consume any decent mother.

"Okay, can you get in touch with the desk sergeant and ask him if he knows anything about the case?"

"I'll get on it now. I'll chase up missing persons, too, see how advanced things were regarding their input."

"Good idea. Let's do all the groundwork this morning and start visiting relatives and friends of the missing girl straight after lunch. What's your gut feeling on this, Lorne?"

She shook her head slowly. "My gut instinct isn't really picking up anything right now, to tell you the truth. Maybe that'll alter as we talk to more people connected with Noelle."

"Let me know what you find out. I better shift some of this lot before I throw myself into the case." Katy held up the pile of post and let it flutter to the desk like autumn leaves. "Come and rescue me in an hour if I haven't surfaced by then, okay?"

"Best of luck with that chore. I'll report back soon."

Lorne sat at her desk in the incident room and rang the desk sergeant to ask if he was aware of the case—he wasn't. Then she rang a contact in the missing person's department. "Debra, it's Lorne. Any chance I can bend your ear for a few seconds?"

"Of course, Lorne. What do you need?"

Lorne gave her friend a brief outline of the case.

"Yes, I remember the case well."

"You do? That's fantastic. What I really want to know is if the parents have been in touch lately to see how things were progressing."

"Funny you should say that. No, they haven't," Debra admitted, a note of sadness evident in her voice.

"Don't you find that kind of strange?"

"Yes and no."

Lorne sighed. "Meaning what exactly? Go on, surprise me."

"The last I heard, Mr. Chesterfield contacted me to say it would be the final call he'd be making."

"Any reason why he should give up so easily?"

"I tried to get the information out of him, but he was very reluctant to answer. Do parents simply give up searching for their daughters like that, Lorne? I know if I ever found myself in that same position, I wouldn't dream of chucking in the towel like that."

"I'm of the same opinion, Debra. Maybe there's an underlying reason the Chesterfields gave up so easily. Anyway, thanks for your help. The inspector and I will be going out to see the parents after lunch. I'll be sure to ask what their reasons were for giving up hope so quickly. If I learn anything of interest, I'll get back to you."

"That'd be great, Lorne. I do so hate these cases left dangling with no resolution."

Lorne hung up and relayed the news to Katy.

"Strange. I'm almost done here."

"Shall I ring the parents and see if it's convenient to see them this morning?" Lorne asked, halfway out the door already.

"You read my mind. Make it about eleven if you can. Maybe we'll sneak in a pub lunch afterwards. How's that?"

"Only if you're paying. I'm skint," Lorne called back over her shoulder.

The butterflies gathered in her tummy as she placed the call. "Is that Mr. Chesterfield?"

A moment's silence greeted her. She almost repeated the question, then finally, the man replied, "Yes, that's me. What do you want? We have double glazing, and we don't need either a new car or a modern kitchen in a sale."

"Glad to hear it," Lorne said light-heartedly. "I'm sorry to disturb you, Mr. Chesterfield. My name is Detective Sergeant Lorne Warner. I'm with the Metropolitan Police. I'm calling to see if it would be convenient for my inspector and me to come and visit you this morning."

"Regarding what?"

Lorne was taken aback by the venom in his words. "Your daughter, Noelle."

Lorne heard the man inhale a large breath when she'd said his daughter's name. The line remained silent for a few seconds.

"Have you found her?" he asked eventually.

The way the man whispered his question made the hairs stand up on the back of her neck and told her how much he cared for his missing daughter in spite of Lorne's misgivings about the parents' lack of pestering the police for any news. "Not yet, Mr. Chesterfield. Your daughter's case is being revisited. Is it possible to drop by this morning about eleven?"

"If you must. I'd like to warn you that my wife has been ill lately and would appreciate it if you'd refrain from building her hopes up about finding Noelle. She's been to hell and back since our daughter disappeared."

"Of course. I can understand that. The last thing we'd want to do is to cause your wife any more heartbreak than she's already experienced, but I think it's essential that we still visit you and run through the details of the case again."

"Very well. Can I ask why the case is being revisited?"

"To be honest, the detectives involved have been suspended, and it's the usual process to go over their cases with a magnifying glass, just to ensure everything was conducted in the proper manner."

Mr. Chesterfield gasped. "You mean Noelle's case was being investigated by incompetent coppers?"

Lorne detected the note of anger. She hadn't intended to rile Mr. Chesterfield before they'd had the chance to run through the case with him and his wife. "We'll go through the details when we arrive, if that's okay with you?"

"Very well. Don't expect an easy ride, Sergeant, will you? If your associates have screwed up, then I'll be looking at chewing the balls off someone to compensate."

"That I can clearly appreciate. All I ask is that you give us a chance to rectify any wrongdoing and to help move the case forward."

"I agree, Sergeant. We'll see you at eleven then." He hung up without giving Lorne the chance to say farewell.

She had a feeling the visit to the Chesterfields' home was going to be a rather prickly one.

CHAPTER TWO

"This is it." Lorne gestured at the detached house tucked away in the corner of the neat residential cul-de-sac in Islington. "That's funny. The first house I owned is just around the corner from here."

"Small world. Okay, let's get this over with."

"They've been through a lot. Let's give them a little slack if they start tearing lumps out of us, agreed?"

"Agreed. To start with, at least. I'm not here to take mountains of crap, though, Lorne. I want to make that clear from the start."

"All right. Let's see how things pan out."

When they got out of the car, the front door of the property opened immediately. An agitated gentleman in his early sixties stood in the doorway, awaiting their arrival.

"Looks like a stormy welcome ahead," Katy said out the corner of her mouth as they approached the house.

The detectives flipped open their ID wallets to introduce themselves. Mr. Chesterfield checked the faces and names thoroughly then stepped back so Lorne and Katy could enter his home.

"I'm Glen, and this is my wife, Diana. This is DI Foster and DS Warner, dear, the ones who called this morning."

"Take a seat, ladies. Would you like a coffee?" The frail-looking woman tried to smile, but the corners of her mouth refused to lift.

"No, thank you," Katy replied, dropping into the sofa at the same time as Lorne. "Mr. Chesterfield has made you aware of why we're here, I take it?"

The woman's terrified gaze connected with her husband's. She reached out a trembling hand for support. Mr. Chesterfield crossed the room and perched on the side of the armchair next to his wife. One hand clutched hers while the other nestled comfortingly around her shaking shoulders. The woman's hands began to tremble more once they were all seated.

"Are you all right, Mrs. Chesterfield? Your husband said you hadn't been too well lately," Lorne said.

"As well as any mother can feel when her child has gone missing," she replied, tears welling up in her sad green eyes.

Mr. Chesterfield pulled a tissue from the box on the side table and handed it to his wife. She smiled weakly at her husband. The gesture broke Lorne's heart. She knew only too well what the pair of them were experiencing after going through a similar ordeal with Charlie over six years ago.

Crap! Where has the time gone? Any mother or father in the same situation would feel the same, wouldn't they? Lorne swallowed the lump that had formed in her throat. "We're aware of how painful our visit is going to be for you, and we're truly sorry about that, but if you'll just bear with us and go through Noelle's case notes, the inspector and I will make sure we do everything to bring a swift conclusion to your daughter's disappearance."

"We're still very bitter about the way the force has treated us, so you'll have to forgive me if you feel the wrath of my sharp tongue during the course of this visit," Mr. Chesterfield said. He squeezed his wife's shoulders then released his arm. Sitting forward, he rested his elbows on his thighs and clenched his hands together.

Lorne let Katy take over asking the questions. "I take it, even before my partner contacted you, you didn't have much confidence in the two officers looking into the case?"

"Not really, Inspector, no."

Lorne took out her notebook while Katy gently urged, "If you felt they weren't doing right by you or your daughter, may I ask why you didn't take your concerns higher, in the form of a complaint?"

Mr. Chesterfield shrugged then stared at the detectives. "Don't your lot usually close ranks? What would have been the point, except to put us through much more heartache than we were already being subjected to?"

"The complaints procedure is there for cases such as this. However, I completely understand your reluctance to go down that route. All I can do is apologise for the way you've been treated. I hope we can right that wrong for you—we certainly intend doing our best," she said compassionately. She cleared her throat then asked, "Can I ask if you've had any form of contact with your daughter since the day she disappeared?"

"No, nothing. As far as we know, none of her friends have heard from her, either. They promised they would ring us right away if she got in touch with them."

"We'll be dropping by her friends—those we're aware of—over the next few days. Did the officers in charge give you any indication of where the case was heading? Give you any hope that they were on to a suspect at all, before they stopped their investigation?" Katy asked tentatively.

"No. I'll be honest with you both. The detectives said they didn't see any reason to keep up the search for Noelle, given her choice of career."

"Working as a pole dancer?"

Mr. Chesterfield sat up and threw an arm around his wife's shoulder when a sob broke from her throat. "Yes. You see, we had no idea at all what Noelle was up to. As far as we were concerned, she went to uni and worked behind a bar part-time at night."

"I'm so sorry. That must have come as an awful shock to learn the truth," Katy said compassionately.

"Yes and no. Our daughter has always stood on her own two feet, never asked us for a penny during her higher education. She was determined to put herself through uni. It wasn't so much her working in the club that upset us. It was the awful way the detectives shared the news with us. I can see the disgusting smirks on their faces even now. How can professionals judge people like that without knowing all the facts? The way they put it across was that Noelle was part of the sex industry, as if she'd been selling her body to all and sundry. Our daughter wouldn't do that, and her friends confirmed she 'never took her work home with her,' but those two morons pressed the idea home to us as though they took pleasure in smearing our daughter's name."

"Again, I can only apologise for their shocking behaviour, as professionals we're taught to handle every case sensitively and not to judge people in any way. I can assure you neither Sergeant Warner nor I will ever tarnish your daughter's name or her choice of career from this day forward. If it's any consolation, I think my former colleagues will rue the day they disrespected not only your daughter's good name but the dozens of other cases we're now being forced to re-open and investigate. If your daughter is out there, we will find her."

"Thank you, Inspector. Your candid assessment is refreshing to hear. I respect you telling it how it is and not hiding the truth. Nowadays, we see very little transparency with issues such as this. We would very much like to put this all behind us and move on. We still believe Noelle is out there somewhere. Her car has never been found. Maybe you could run that through your police system again?"

"We'll definitely be doing that, Mr. Chesterfield. Today, our main goal was to come out and introduce ourselves and to assure you that we will be taking your daughter's disappearance seriously. We wanted to do this before we started the investigation from scratch— we think that will be the best way, considering how crass and inept our former colleagues seem to have been during the search for clues."

"Then we're happy for you to contact us to ask whatever you need to ask. All we want is for Noelle to be returned to us. Do you think one of the men visiting the club might have abducted her? That's always been at the back of our minds."

"It's possible, Mr. Chesterfield. Let's face it—anything is possible in this day and age," Katy said. "What I foresee hampering us is the fact that Noelle has been missing for six months. Nevertheless, if there is a clue to be found, my resourceful team will find it. I don't suppose Noelle could have gone away to relatives, could she?"

Lorne gave a slight cough and shook her head. "Just to recap, Inspector, Noelle was on her way to stay with her friend, Abbie."

"That's right, silly me. We'll be contacting Abbie today to verify the conversation she had with Noelle before her disappearance," Katy accepted Lorne's interruption gracefully.

"That's right. Noelle just wanted to get away from her flat, Inspector. We begged her to come here, we were on holiday at the time, but maybe she felt it wouldn't be wise putting us in harm's way. She never really did tell us why she decided not to stay here when she called to tell us about the incident at her flat. Like I've said already, maybe her stubbornness and determination to be independent forced her hand on her decision-making process. Who knows what went on in our daughter's pretty head, sometimes?" Mr. Chesterfield smiled fondly at the photo hanging on the wall above the mantelpiece.

"Okay. Why don't we leave it there for now? I want to reassure you that from this day on, your daughter will be at the top of our priority list. Do you have any questions for us?"

The couple looked at each other. Then Mr. Chesterfield said, "Just one."

"Go on?" Katy asked with a smile.

"Do you have any children, Inspector?"

Katy shook her head. "No, Mr. Chesterfield, but my partner has, and she will be working alongside me at all times, keeping me in line. I'm sure she won't mind me confiding in you that her own daughter was abducted a few years ago. She fought like a lioness to get her daughter back in one piece, even defying orders from above. To me, you could have no one better fighting in your corner on this one."

Katy winked at Lorne, and she felt her cheeks flood with heat. "My daughter was found safe and well, Mr. and Mrs. Chesterfield. Let's hope the same fate is awaiting Noelle."

"We appreciate your openness. It can't be easy working on a case so close to something that has touched your own family, Sergeant. I hope it doesn't bring back too many bad memories for you."

"I have no doubt it will stir up terrible memories. However, the fact I still have my daughter will help to overcome them. I give you my word that we'll do everything we can to ensure you have the same outcome. Our children are special gifts that no one has the right to tear from our lives."

"Thank you, Sergeant."

As Lorne and Katy stood up to leave, Mrs. Chesterfield looked at them and pleaded, "Please bring her home. She's our only child, our life. Without her, there really is no need for us to go on."

Lorne got down on one knee and clasped Mrs. Chesterfield's hand. "You've found the courage to stay strong this far. Dig deep and search for the strength to continue. You have my assurance that we'll do all we can to pick out the trail of where Noelle is. If she is still out there, we'll bring her back home to you."

Tears trickled from Mrs. Chesterfield's eyes and teetered on her cheek. "Thank you."

At the front door, Mr. Chesterfield looked over his shoulder at the living room door they'd just exited. "My wife blames herself for our daughter's disappearance," he said quietly. "Don't ask me why. I suppose every mother would do the same thing. She's on medication for depression. I have to keep the tablets locked away. If I didn't, I think she might have ended her life months ago. I believe your visit today has given her hope, something to cling to. I'm grateful for that, and for you taking up our daughter's case when we believed the police had forgotten her."

Lorne rubbed her hand up and down his arm. "You need to not only take care of your wife but of yourself, too. A word of caution, if

I may? You need to prepare yourself for a bad outcome, given the length of time it's been since Noelle was reported missing."

"I'm not silly, Sergeant. I realise what the odds are and that they're not in our favour. We just want her back, alive or…"

Everyone standing in the confines of the tiny hallway knew what he meant. Lorne and Katy shook his hand and left the house. Back in the car, they each let out a huge sigh.

"Those poor people. How could Travers and Campbell do this to them?" Lorne shook her head.

Katy started the engine. "And they say most criminals are sick in the head. If that's the case, what does that make these two morons? This is just one case, remember? Look at the devastation their corrupt ways have brought on all the other lives involved in the cases being reinvestigated."

"My thoughts exactly. Are we still going to have lunch out? I'd like to take an in-depth look at the file, see if there's anything obvious we're missing while we eat."

"Yep, sounds like a plan to me. How about the Packhorse, the new pub that's had the classy refit recently? It's close to the station, too."

Lorne nodded. "I've been meaning to check out that place. The initial reports about their food appear to be good."

Twenty minutes later, Katy arrived at the pub to find punters already making their way inside the thatched black-and-white public house. They both ordered cod and chips. While she and Katy waited for the meals to arrive, Lorne bought two orange juices from the bar. Katy flipped open the file, and they silently surveyed its contents for a few minutes.

"Unbelievable. What the hell?" Lorne said.

"What? I take it you're talking about the lack of witness accounts?"

Lorne took a sip from her glass. "Too bloody right. This case looks as though it was treated like some kind of joke from the very first day. Why? Because of where she worked?"

"You could be right. We'll make amends, Lorne. We have to."

The waitress appeared with two plates heaped with chips and battered cod. After the waitress deposited the meals and left, Katy continued, "We're going to start from scratch. How about we work late tonight and pay the club where she worked a visit, to see what the staff have to say?"

"Fine by me. I'll have to contact Tony to let him know I'll be late home, but I don't foresee a problem."

"That's settled then. Let's tuck in—it might be the last meal we get this side of tomorrow."

Lorne stepped outside and sat on one of the kiddie swings in the adventure playground area at the rear of the pub. As she dialled Tony's mobile, the thought crossed her mind to play a practical joke on him—something along the lines of putting on a voice and pretending to be a damsel in distress. Then she remembered that her number would show up on his screen. "Hi, Tony. How's the investigation going?"

"Hi. Slowly, in a word. I was just thinking about you."

"You were? Why? Keep it clean. I'm in a kiddie's play area."

Tony laughed. "I didn't know they had a crèche at the station. Mind you, looking at the age of some of the force's latest recruits, I can totally see the need for installing one."

"Idiot! Katy and I are having lunch out. Umm… you know when I said I wouldn't volunteer for any overtime when I rejoined the force…"

"Yes," he replied, sounding suspicious.

"Well, I lied. I shouldn't be that late, I promise."

"Is this to do with a new case?" Tony asked then let out a sigh.

"Yep, it's a cold case. We've just visited the parents, and well, it was heart-breaking, brought back so many tortured memories of what happened to Charlie. I have to give this case my all, if only for them, love."

"No need to apologise or make excuses, hon. I totally understand. Are you going to tell me what the case is?"

"In a nutshell, a young girl went missing six months ago. This case belonged to two bent coppers, and it's one of many being revisited. By what we've gleaned so far, they didn't exactly put themselves out to investigate the bloody case because the girl was paying for uni by working at a pole dancers' club."

"Crap. All right, you do what you have to do and just come home safely, okay?"

"Will do. Love you." Lorne hung up and joined Katy in the car.

"Everything okay?"

"Yep, he's fine. I feel pretty shit going back on my word never to work extended hours, though."

Katy turned her head sharply to look at her. "Did he throw that at you?"

"No. He was really supportive, as always. It's just me and my guilt gene pricking my conscience. Back to the station now?"

"Yep, let's see if the team have managed to come up with anything while we've been out."

"You forgot to add stuffing our faces." Lorne laughed.

Katy cringed. "Do you think we should stop off en route and pick them up some sandwiches?"

"Good idea."

Once they arrived in the office, Lorne handed out the sandwiches they'd just bought to the grateful team then moved over to the incident board.

AJ was the first to speak. "I've done my usual trick of chasing up the CCTV footage from the cameras in the vicinity of the club. Hope that was okay?"

"Brilliant. Are they likely to go that far back?" Katy pulled out a chair alongside Lorne and sat down.

"Yep, they should go back at least twelve months," AJ confirmed with a smile.

Lorne jotted that task on the board then wrote down the word *car*. "Any news on the vehicle? Maybe we should check if it's still registered in Noelle's name, yes?"

Karen Titchard raised her hand. "I'll look into that after lunch. While you were out, I checked the witnesses' addresses, made sure they were up to date. I thought you'd want to start questioning them soon."

"Thanks, Karen. Any we need to chase up?"

"The few that were on file still live at the same address. There weren't that many, though, were there?" Karen replied, shaking her head ruefully.

"That's a huge disappointment to us. Lorne and I are planning to work overtime tonight to visit the club. Hopefully, we'll be able to get a clearer picture of what actually went on that night or if there were any problems down there during the nights before the incident. The file mentions that Noelle said there was an incident in the alley behind the club the night before she found the intruder in her apartment—she thought someone might have been following her.

Maybe someone saw something that night. We'll see. Places like this tend to treat the police with disrespect." Katy shrugged. "What else have we got?"

Lorne scribbled on the board as she spoke. "Well, we've seen the parents. We should visit the neighbours, ask if they saw anyone suspicious lingering around the property at that time. There's also Noelle's friend Abbie, whom she was planning on staying with. Perhaps she can give us a little more background information into Noelle's past relationships. She was obviously a good friend if Noelle was on her way over there to stay with her."

Katy nodded and addressed the team, "Any objections to me sending a few of you guys out to question some of these folks? I'm hoping to tie up this case ASAP. Can anyone think of any other avenues we should be exploring?"

"What about looking into possible complaints from other members of the staff working at the club?" Graham Barlow called out. "If we're looking at the incidents being connected."

Lorne noted how tired the young detective looked, and she made a mental note to pull him aside after the meeting to see if everything was okay at home. He'd taken on a lot for someone his age. At twenty-sixish, the detective had already been married for four years and was the proud father to two children under the age of three. Lorne was full of admiration for anyone taking on that kind of challenge in today's world. Graham and his wife, Liz, were childhood sweethearts, and from the time they'd got together, they had meticulously planned out their lives. They were married at twenty-one and had all the children they wanted by the age of twenty-five. That way, when they'll be in their early forties, having done their duty of bringing up the kids, they could go on to thoroughly enjoy what remained of their lives. One day over coffee, Graham had confided in Lorne that travelling the world was high up on their agenda. Maybe the pressure he'd put himself under was starting to get to him, if the worry lines on his young features were anything to go by.

Katy smiled at him. "Great idea, Graham. Lorne and I can look into that side of things before we set off for the club later. Anything else?"

The team responded with shaking heads.

"Okay, Stephen and Graham, I'd like you to get in touch with the witnesses, on the friends and family side of things, and organise dropping by for a quick chat to go over the facts. Leave the witnesses from the club for Lorne and me to chase up, okay?"

"Yes, boss," the two detectives said in unison.

"AJ and Karen, I think you're both better suited to working around here. AJ, once you get hold of the CCTV discs, I'd like you to search through them see what you can come up with. And, Karen, keep on the vehicle side of things. I'd also like you to contact the media, TV and radio, and make them aware of the case and the urgency to bring it to a conclusion."

"Okay. Shall I ring the BBC? Maybe pursue a slot on *Crimewatch*? Perhaps they'll consider doing a reconstruction of the crime," Karen suggested.

"Why not? It can't hurt, although I'm not sure how many people, er… sober people would be around at the time of morning Noelle left work. It's definitely worth a shot."

Karen chuckled. "I see what you mean. Maybe it would be better to do a reconstruction consisting of the attack at her home rather than her activities at the club. The intruder broke in during the daylight hours, didn't he?"

Katy clicked her fingers. "Spot on. Good thinking, Karen. Anything else? Okay, then let's get to work, people. Report back with any significant findings as they come your way, please."

Lorne and Katy went through to her office. "Do you want me to collate what we have regarding the staff at the club and see if any of them have connections to other crimes?" Lorne asked before either of them had a chance to sit down.

"Sounds good to me. I'll be busy doing my usual mountaineering trick of combating my post in the meantime. I've still got a few loose ends I need to tie into a pretty bow regarding the case we solved last week, too, before Roberts comes after me for my blood."

"Talking of Roberts…" Lorne said, lowering her voice and pushing the door closed with her fingertips. "Have you heard anything about a possible move on the cards for him in the pipeline?"

Katy frowned. "Should I? Has he hinted at anything of that nature?"

"Yes and no. Oh, just ignore me, maybe it's something in the air. Graham looks as though he has the weight of the world on his shoulders at the moment, too. Mind if I have a quick chat with him before he gets stuck into his tasks?"

"Sure. We need to know what's going on with him and if it's likely to affect his work. Regarding Roberts, I hope you're wrong about him moving on. I know he pushes me and can be a severe pain in the arse at times, but I'd rather have him tear me off a strip than an outsider any day."

Lorne nodded in agreement. "Yep, likewise. I know all about superiors being a pain in the arse, too." She winked at Katy and bolted out of the office before her colleague could launch a missile at her.

She tapped Graham's shoulder and pulled up a chair to sit alongside him. "How's it going?"

He looked down at the notes he'd been scribbling then back at her.

Lorne shook her head. "Not with the case. I mean with you in general. Tell me to keep my nose out if you like, but you look exhausted."

His shoulders slumped, and he reclined in his chair. "Is it that obvious? I thought I was hiding it well."

"To me, yes. I'm the one around here who has the near worn out T-shirt with the motto 'Been there, done that, here's the T-shirt to prove it.' Want to share? Not the T-shirt. I was referring to what's bothering you?"

"Thanks, Lorne. One word pretty much sums it all up—*pregnant*!"

Her mouth momentarily dropped open, then she closed it again. "No, seriously? Liz is pregnant *again*?"

He tried to force a smile, but Lorne could tell what a heavy burden just saying the word aloud was to the young man. She reached out and rubbed his forearm. "I thought you only had plans for two kids?"

"We did. Don't get me wrong, Kiki and Maria are mine and Liz's world. It's just…"

"The shock will pass, and you'll get accustomed to the idea of being a dad again soon, Graham. I'm sure you will. How does Liz feel about the news?"

"She's as devastated as I am. Not that we'd ever think of getting rid of it," Graham added quickly.

"I'm sure you wouldn't. Just give it time, hon. You're still what? Twenty-six or twenty-seven?"

"Twenty-five."

Lorne cringed at the thought of having to personally deal with three kids under the age of four at his age. There's just no way she would have ever coped if the situation had landed on her doorstep. "Do you have any holidays due?"

"Next month. Why?"

"Well, my suggestion is to leave your two adorable girls with your family and take off somewhere, just you and Liz, even if it's only for a weekend. Things will look so much brighter once you've thrashed out the details and had time to get used to the idea."

"That's what my mum also suggested. She's volunteered to look after the kids for us. The odds on getting a weekend off now, though, seems pretty remote with all this crap landing on us, doesn't it?"

"Nonsense, we're a crack team. We should have all this cleared up in a few weeks. There's nothing to stop you taking off then, is there?"

He sniggered. "Knowing my luck, another big murder case will come crashing down on my desk before I get the chance to even book the hotel room."

Lorne tapped his arm. "Stop being so negative."

"That's easy for you to say. How many kids have you got?"

"Just the one. I knew from the very first day I held my daughter that she would be an only child." She leaned in to whisper, "I admire you more than you could ever know, Graham. I would never have the patience for bringing up more than one child."

"You're not the only one to tell me that. It's tougher than most people think, but Liz and I have coped all right with the situation, up until now. Her announcement last night was like a sucker punch to the gut, though. The thing that's really tearing me apart is the fact I feel guilty."

"Guilty? For what?"

"For feeling so devastated and not elated by the news. It's not the foetus's fault. It's mine and Liz's for not taking more care." His cheeks coloured up, and his gaze dropped to the desk.

"There's no need to be embarrassed admitting that. It's refreshing for you to reveal it, to be honest. Most men wouldn't, but you're different from most men, Graham. You've already proven that by getting married and starting a family so young. Like I've said already, go away and sit down with Liz and *talk*."

He glanced up and smiled at Lorne. "Thanks. I appreciate you going out of your way to ask and listen to my troubles."

"Anytime. I'm always here, and my shoulder has gone through some soggy times over the years, I can assure you. In the end, you have to listen to both your heart and your head on this matter, Graham. You and Liz will do the right thing. Hey, look at it this way, you have nine months to get used to the idea."

"Wrong! That'll be seven and a half months, to be exact." He smiled for the first time that morning, showing off his perfectly white teeth.

She rose from her seat and tweaked his cheek. "I'm always here for you." Lorne returned to her desk with a glowing heat surrounding her heart, feeling good that Graham had opened up. She flipped open the case file and noted down the names of the people they needed to interview at the club. Then she searched the police system for any possible incidents that had occurred at the address. According to the records, the club had held its licence for only two years, and in that time, the club had seen very little trouble that had led the police to the door. She then went on to search the database for any crimes apportioned to the witnesses—the other dancers at the club—and results were insignificant.

Within an hour, Stephen and Graham had left the station to do the necessary house-to-house enquiries surrounding Noelle's home, and Karen had reported the results of the car investigations. According to DVLA, the car was still registered in Noelle's name.

Lorne tapped her chin thoughtfully with a pen. "Interesting. We should put out a bulletin, get the squad cars to keep their eyes peeled for the car. What do you think?"

"I'll get onto it now," Karen said. "Oh, and by the way, *Crimewatch* are going to sort out a reconstruction to air on the show next week."

"That's brilliant. Can I leave you to supply them with all the relevant details they need, Karen?"

"My pleasure." Karen smiled and turned back to her computer.

Katy came out of her office, looking fed up and ripe for doing serious harm to anyone who pissed her off. "How's it going?"

Lorne smiled and told her where they stood with the investigation.

"Good. I think you and I should get out of here, see how many of Noelle's friends we can interview before we call at the club. I want to be there around nine or thereabouts."

"Okay. I'll gather the addresses and be with you in five minutes."

CHAPTER THREE

At almost five o'clock, Lorne and Katy approached the terraced house in the quiet street. Abbie Ball opened the door and invited them into her living room.

"Thanks for agreeing to see us at such short notice, Miss Ball." Katy smiled at the young blonde woman, who, judging by the dark rings around her eyes, hadn't slept much lately.

"Anything I can do to help, Inspector? You only have to ask."

Katy sat forward and placed her elbows on her knees. "We've just reopened Noelle's case and wondered if you would be kind enough to go through the events leading up to her disappearance? Are you up to that?"

"I think so. I had some bad news a few days ago that, to be honest, has rocked my world. I'm not really thinking straight at the moment, but I'll do my best."

Katy and Lorne glanced at each other.

Then Katy asked, "Is there something we can do to help on that front?"

"Not unless you're a heart surgeon. My dad has to have a triple heart bypass in the next few months."

"I'm sorry to hear that. I'm sure things will turn out for the best."

"I hope so. Sorry, you were asking about Noelle. Can I ask why the case has been reopened after all this time? I thought you guys had forgotten about her by now."

Katy sighed. "Well, it's come to our attention that the case wasn't dealt with appropriately by the previous detectives, and head office have issued instructions for us to look into the case thoroughly. I take it you haven't heard from Noelle since she was reported missing?"

"No. Not at all. She just vanished. The minute I got the phone call saying she was on her way over here, I jumped into action and threw clean sheets on the spare bed. It's still made up for her now. How can someone just disappear like that? Do you think the guy in the flat abducted her?"

"Until we interview all the witnesses, we'd rather not draw any conclusions, Abbie. What we do know is that we have far too many unanswered questions that we need to get answers to. Was Noelle single?"

"Yes. She broke up with Danny long before this happened."

"Did she break up with him, or was it the other way round?" Katy asked.

"She broke it off with him. Said he was a little too possessive."

Katy raised her eyebrow at Lorne. "Were they dating for long? Did he know what type of career she had?"

"I think a year in total, on and off. They fell out a lot, and yes, that was due to her working at the club."

"I see. I don't suppose you have a full name and address for him, do you?"

Abbie went to a desk in the corner. She rummaged through the top drawer and pulled out a small flowered address book. "Here we are. Danny Smalling. The only address I have for him is this one." Abbie handed the book to Lorne, who jotted down the information in her notebook.

"Have you seen him recently?"

Abbie returned to her seat and shook her head. "No, not that I had much to do with him anyway. He always gave off a nasty vibe. I got the impression that he wanted Noelle to break contact with me. Not just me, either. Other friends I've spoken to since got the same impression."

"Can you think of anything else or anyone else we should be looking into?" Katy asked.

"Not really. To be honest, Noelle didn't tend to share the experiences she had at the club with me. It was kind of an unspoken understanding that the topic was best avoided by both of us."

Katy stood, and Lorne followed, tucking her notebook away. "You've been really helpful. We're going to leave now, see if we can track this Danny down as soon as possible. I hope your dad recovers well from his operation. Keep the faith where Noelle is concerned, too, all right? You have our word that if she's still out there, we will do our utmost to bring her back home to you all." Katy gave the young woman a business card.

"Thank you. If I hear from Noelle, I'll be sure to ring you. Fingers crossed you're successful in your mission. I miss her terribly."

Lorne and Katy said farewell and jumped back in the car. Before Katy started the engine, she turned to Lorne. "Do you remember seeing anything in the case file about a boyfriend?"

Lorne clenched her teeth and shook her head. "Nope. What the fuck was wrong with those guys? That should have been their first port of call. What's the betting he's no longer living at this address, either?"

"Only one way to find out." Katy input the address into the sat nav then set the car in motion. "Why is it that other people's stupid mistakes always land on our bloody desks?"

"That's a bit of an exaggeration, but I get your drift. It does beggar belief, given what the statistics say about the first twenty-four hours of someone going missing being the most important. Bloody men!"

"Thankfully, you and I both know that some of them think like us. We're lucky to have found Tony and AJ. They're definitely the exception to the rule."

"You mean we've knocked them into shape nicely." Lorne chuckled.

"My sentiments exactly. The address we're after is about twenty minutes from here. Let's hope it doesn't turn out to be a waste of time."

The ex-boyfriend's house was situated in one of the less-inviting suburbs of the city. Lorne rapped on the front door. She didn't care to take a chance of ringing the bell, which was hanging off the frame, its wires exposed to the elements.

Eventually, after several fraught minutes, the door opened to reveal a young man in his early twenties in desperate need of a haircut and a shave. "Yeah, what d'ya want? I'm busy."

Katy produced her ID. "DI Katy Foster and my partner, DS Lorne Warner. Are you Danny Smalling?"

The man's lip turned up at the side, and his eyes narrowed. "Why?"

"*Are you* Danny Smalling? It's a simple enough question." Katy repeated while Lorne got ready to pounce if the youngster decided to slam the door in their faces.

"It depends."

"Cut the crap. We don't have time. Are you Danny Smalling, yes or no? Either you answer me now, or we'll take you down the station and charge you for trying to pervert the course of justice. You hear me?"

Lorne could see the man's arm shift behind the pane of glass, and she lunged forward. "No you don't, smartarse. Now, answer the damn question."

"No. I mean, no—I ain't Danny. You've got no right to turn up here like this and treat me this way. My dad's a barrister, and I'll make sure he wipes the floor with you for harassing me like this."

"Really? His name? We're quite friendly with all the barristers in the area. If you're not Danny, why didn't you just tell us that from the start?"

"Because you didn't give me a chance."

"Right! Okay, let's see some form of ID then."

His eyes widened in disbelief. "Why? What the fuck have I done now?"

Katy smiled tightly and shooed him with her hands. "Hop to it. You can leave the door open."

The youngster looked Lorne up and down. "Like I have a choice with her standing right there."

He left the front door and went back into the flat on the ground floor. An eternity seemed to pass before he reappeared, carrying his passport. Katy snatched it from his grasp.

"Taylor Munroe, it would be wise of you in the future not to meddle with police officers. Not all of them are as kind-hearted as me and the sergeant here. Where's Danny then?"

"How the fuck should I know?"

"Less of the language. Do you know him well?"

"Not at all. When I moved in, the bedsit was empty, had been for at least a month."

"How long ago was that?" Katy asked.

"About four months ago, I think. Why? What's he done?"

Katy tilted her head. "What makes you think he's done anything wrong?"

"Doh, let me consider that for a mo. Oh yeah, you're both coppers, go figure!"

"You've got a smart mouth for someone whose dad is in the same line of business as us."

Munroe chortled and leaned back casually against the wall. "Hardly, but I get your drift. Come on, what's this guy done wrong?"

"Nothing. We just wanted a brief chat with him about something. Any chance of you bumping into him?" Katy pressed.

"Nope. Our paths haven't crossed at all. Mind if I get on now?"

"Thanks for talking to us, eventually. See, it was painless in the end."

As Lorne and Katy headed back to the car, the door slammed behind them.

"Jumped-up prick," Katy mumbled.

"We probably interfered with his gaming session on the X-Box," Lorne said sarcastically.

They both continued to chuckle until they reached the Tickle Club. Katy parked in the club's car park and switched off the engine. "Looks like we're a bit early. Should we wait out here for a while or go in?"

"Not sure the manager or the staff will appreciate us arriving when they're setting up, but then on the other hand, we'll probably get more out of them with no punters around." Lorne pulled on the handle and stepped out of the car. She looked down at the black suit she wore. "One look at us, and they'll know we're not there for the entertainment."

"That's true enough. Let's go piss off some people. Don't forget to smile now."

There was no bouncer on duty at the door, so they had no problem entering the club. They didn't come across any form of life until they reached the bar area. The beat of the music vibrated across the floor and tickled the bottom of Lorne's feet through the soles of her shoes. A black-haired girl in her early twenties, wearing a low-cut top that left very little to the imagination, stood behind the highly polished mahogany bar, waiting for them to approach.

"What can I get you, ladies?" Her taut smile forced her lips apart to show glistening teeth that sparkled under the bar's lights.

Both detectives flashed their IDs. "A word with the manager would be great," Katy said, returning the barmaid's tight smile.

"He's busy at the moment. I'll tell him you're here, though. Be right back."

Lorne and Katy watched her leave the bar through a door at the back. They walked past the bar and snooped around the main seating area surrounding the stage in the middle of the room. Sitting in the front row were a group of university-aged youngsters, giggling and high-fiving each other whilst they waited in anticipation of the show.

"Wonder if their parents know what they get up to when they should be doing homework for their studies?" Lorne leaned over and said loud enough for Katy to hear above the music.

Before Katy could answer, a tall man sporting a goatee and a rounded beer belly greeted them. "Ladies. What can I do for you?"

After they had flashed their warrant cards again, Katy asked, "Is there somewhere quiet we can talk, Mr…?"

The man frowned. "It's Norton, Ken Norton. About what? You are aware that this place is about to get exceptionally busy in about half an hour?"

"We'll try not to hold you up too long. It's about one of your former employees, Noelle Chesterfield."

His frown deepened. "Noelle? Has she turned up after all this time?"

"No. We've taken over the investigation, revisiting and questioning again colleagues and family, hoping to find some new clues," Katy said to the manager. "Now, do you have an office where we can talk privately?"

"I can spare you five minutes, I suppose. Doubt if I can tell you anything different to what I told the other detectives. Come with me."

Lorne and Katy followed him through a narrow corridor decorated with posters of nearly naked girls, most of them skinnier than a starving dog, but Lorne spotted a couple of girls who actually carried a few excess pounds. *Catering for different clientele, I guess.*

The office was a tip, cluttered with rails of costumes and T-shirts emblazoned with the club's logo across the front and boxes spilling advertising leaflets over the stained grey carpet.

Lorne shuddered at the thought of working in such a confined space, fearing that claustrophobia could strike any moment.

Katy didn't waste any time asking her first question while Lorne prepared to note down Norton's answers. "Can you tell us what happened during Noelle's last shift at the club?"

"The normal—she turned up, danced, and left. It's the same answer I gave last time. Nothing has changed."

"I know this is strange, Mr. Norton, but please bear with us. The reason we've reopened the case is because the original detectives are on suspension."

"Whoa, bent coppers. Who'd have thunk it!" He roared with laughter, leaned back in his chair, placed both legs on his desk, and crossed his ankles.

"I never said they were bent. Going back to that night—can you tell me if Noelle had any problems with any of your customers?"

He pondered the question for several seconds before responding. "Problems? Apart from the normal behaviour our girls are subjected to?"

Katy tilted her head. "Depends what you're referring to as normal, Mr. Norton?"

"Well, sure they get heckled, and most nights, some idiots try to cop a feel, but the security guys take care of clowns indulging in those antics. Cut the crap before it gets a chance to escalate."

"And did someone try to 'cop a feel' that night during Noelle's performance?"

He hitched up one shoulder. "Not that I'm aware. Mind you, it was my night off. I had a date with a hot bird."

Katy blew out a breath. "Who do you leave in charge on your nights off?"

"My assistant manager. I'm training him up. He's just out of nappies. Thought he'd grow up quicker in these surroundings than standing around, pulling pints behind a regular bar, deluded idiot."

"This assistant, does he have a name?"

"Ty Dolan. He's on duty now. You can't talk to him until he's finished in the cellar, though. I need those kegs attached and ready for when the punters want to spend their dosh."

"We're willing to wait for the right information. Do you have CCTV footage at the club?"

"Outside, yes. Not really inside, if that's what you're getting at. I think your lot took a copy of the discs. Didn't they hand them in?"

"I'll delve into that when we get back to the station," Katy said. "Will it be convenient for us to question some of the girls, or all of the girls on duty that night?"

"If you must. You'll have to make it quick. I do have a business to run, ladies, as I'm sure you can appreciate."

"We do. If you can't add anything further about that night, maybe we can speak to some of the girls while we wait for Mr. Dolan to become free?"

"Sure." He removed his legs from the desk and stood up. "I'll take you into the dressing room. A word of warning—some of the girls won't take kindly to the intrusion at this time of night."

"We're prepared to take that risk in order to get the answers we need to help find Noelle, Mr. Norton."

He tutted, and the three of them left the office and entered the adjoining door on the right. The instant they stepped into the room, Lorne felt every eye turn their way. Some of the looks dished out by the half-clothed girls were enough to put the fear of God into anyone other than Lorne or Katy, who succeeded in combatting the evil stares with their disarming smiles.

"Listen up, girls. These detectives are here to ask you all some questions about Noelle Chesterfield. Let's do what we can to help, okay?" Norton nodded at Lorne and Katy and left the room.

Some of the girls began circling the detectives as if they were some kind of prey, but neither Lorne nor Katy flinched or offered the girls any fear to feed on.

"We're only interested in the girls on duty during Noelle's last shift."

The only noise that filled the room was the music from outside. Then one of the smaller girls moved between Lorne and Katy. "I was here that night," she said, jerking a thumb at her chest.

"And you are?" Lorne asked, taking the notebook from her pocket.

"Calinda Foxton."

"Do you want to run through what happened that night? I mean, do you recall if anything out of the ordinary occurred that night?"

"Thinking back, I seem to recall something. Give me a minute or so, will you?"

"Take your time, Calinda," Katy said, smiling.

"Not too long, Cal. You're up first, remember?" one of the other girls reminded her.

"Crap, so I am." She clicked her fingers. "Usually, the punters generally behave themselves. Of course, we get the odd tosser who chances his arm, but mostly, our crowd know what's expected of them."

"Which is?" Katy asked.

"To watch and not tamper with the girls. Well, I think there were two or three guys who set out to bend the rules that night. Most of us were back here at the time. Noelle was on stage, doing her act. She was great at her job, got the most tips out of all of us. Anyway, I think the security had to throw one of the guys out for jumping on the stage." She paused to search her memory.

Katy prompted the young beauty to continue, "And?"

"Well, while the heavies were escorting the guy out, two other men jumped up on stage and started touching Noelle up. She screamed, but by the time help arrived, the two men had pawed and grabbed at every inch of her. She managed to get away and ran back here to escape them. She was pretty shaken up, too."

"Did she go home?"

"No. She stayed until the end of the shift. We did our best to make light of the event, and by the time she left that night, she was virtually back to her old spunky self. Noelle really wasn't one for taking crap from the customers."

"No one thought to leave with her? Just in case one of the men who groped her was waiting outside for her to leave?" Katy asked, scanning the crowd.

Many of the women bowed their heads and avoided eye contact.

"Wait a minute, we've all got our own lives to lead. I think the security guys watched her from the back door for a while. You'll need to ask them that question. It ain't our job to look out for one another once we're off the premises."

Katy nodded. "Okay, we'll have a word with the security guys. Maybe if there is any kind of trouble in the future, you guys should consider leaving this place in pairs for safety reasons."

"Whatever," a pretty black girl called out from the back of the group.

Katy took a few paces towards the woman. "Doesn't my suggestion make sense?"

The woman shrugged her slender shoulders, folded her arms across her scrawny chest tucked into a gold-lamé bikini top, and turned her head away. "Like I said, whatever. In case you ain't noticed, honey, we don't work in a toy shop! Weirdoes kind of come with the territory."

The other girls mumbled in agreement.

Lorne frowned. "Which is why you should reconsider your regime at the end of your shift and look out for one another as the inspector just pointed out."

The woman laughed. "It ain't always that simple. Anyways, you're wasting your time."

"We are?" Katy asked with a frown of her own set firmly in place.

"Yeah. If Noelle was abducted or attacked after her shift, then fair enough, but if my memory is correct, she wasn't. Didn't she go missing a day or two after her last shift here?"

"You're right. But someone attacked her at her flat before she was abducted. And, given her choice of career, it seems likely that the person who attacked Noelle at her home could have followed her home from here. All we're trying to do is make a possible link. Maybe that was their intention, not to make a move that night, to avoid any awkward questions from the police. Have you thought about it that way?"

Silence filled the room and eyes looked away from Katy.

"Look, I don't want to come across heavy-handed, ladies. All we're trying to do is find out the actual facts of what went on during Noelle's last shift. Is there anything else you think we should know about these men? Can anyone put a name to any of these men, for instance? Anything at all would help at this stage of the enquiry."

Calinda spoke up for the group after a moment's hesitation. "Gary, I think I heard one of the security guys call one of them. Ask them, they'll tell you. I need to get ready now." She waited for Lorne to dismiss her.

"We really appreciate your help. I'll leave a card for each of you, and if anything else comes to mind, please contact me. Day or night, okay?"

Katy and Lorne left the dressing room. By the time they walked back into the bar area, the place was almost full.

"Jesus! This place fills up quickly—early, too," Lorne stated. "I was thinking back there, you don't suppose one of the other girls could be behind Noelle's disappearance?"

"Why do you say that, Lorne?" Katy asked, casting a watchful eye on the customers.

"Well, they all seemed a little sheepish when Calinda mentioned that Noelle was popular and that she obtained more tips than anyone else. That could be seen as a motive. Envy can be a dangerous motivation, as we've both witnessed over the years."

"Maybe you're onto something. I'll track down the manager and see if I can get the girls' details while you have a natter with the security blokes. How's that?"

"Makes sense. I'll keep an eye on the punters at the same time. We stick out like walking beacons in this place—that's bound to spook anyone with a guilty conscience."

"Be back in a few minutes." Katy turned and walked towards the manager's office.

Lorne tucked herself behind a large column and discreetly surveyed the excited crowd. A shudder ran through her when she realised how respectable the patrons seemed. She hadn't really known what to expect because she hadn't visited many clubs before. She didn't see anyone who looked like an obvious weirdo, despite what the dancers had said. *Maybe the real misbehaving happens once the entertainment begins and the instincts take over?* After locating two security men wearing black suits lingering by the bar, she crossed the room to talk to them.

The giants glanced down at her five-six frame with amusement stretching across their scarred features. She quickly flashed her ID and tucked her warrant card back in her pocket, hoping none of the customers noticed. Standing inches in front of the men, she beckoned them to lean in, so she could be heard above the music, which had been ramped up in the last few seconds, intimating that the start of the show was imminent.

"I'm here with my colleague—she's in there talking to the manager now—and we're investigating a missing person. Noelle Chesterfield. Do you remember her?"

"Yeah, I remember her. She was a beautiful girl, smart kid. Dave wasn't here then," the older of the two men replied.

"Great, and you are?"

"Mitch Edmonds."

"Nice to meet you, Mitch. I've just been talking to the dancers, and they told me there was a bit of trouble during Noelle's last shift. Can you shed any light on that?"

Mitch's head bounced up and down as if he were a puppet on a string. "Yeah, there was a bit of bother that night, unusual for around here. Our presence usually deters the punters from overstepping the mark. Not sure what happened that night. Things seemed to get out of control quickly."

"Do you know the names of any of the men involved in the commotion?"

"I seem to recall Gary chanced his arm that night. He's a regular. He's not all there. Reckon he's got more than a dozen screws loose, that one."

Lorne noted the name in her notebook. "I don't suppose you have a surname or a possible address for this Gary?"

"Christ, lady. You don't expect much, do ya?"

"Worth a try." She shrugged. "He's a regular, you say? Do you have some kind of membership at this club? Would his details be on record somewhere perhaps?"

"Nah, we don't hand out memberships. They just come and go as they please as long as they can afford to pay the entrance fee."

"Which is?" Lorne asked, raising a questioning eyebrow.

"Thirty quid. Not that expensive, given the talent on show." He dug his colleague in the ribs and laughed raucously.

"That seems pretty darn expensive to me. If, as you say, this Gary has learning difficulties, how does he come up with the entrance fee, do you suppose?"

"Did I say he had learning difficulties?"

"You mentioned he has a screw loose. Were you indicating something else then?" Lorne asked.

"All right, you've got me there. Listen..." He moved in closer. "Some of the guys feel sorry for him and allow him in for nothing."

Lorne's eyes bulged. "You're kidding me? Do you recognise how irresponsible that is?"

The brute shrugged, and his lip curled up. "Hey, call it community service. Guys like that need to get their kicks somehow. They're not likely to get their hands on any real pussy anytime soon if we don't lend them a helping hand."

Lorne was appalled by the man's admission. She shook her head in disgust. "So, if you're doing him this *big* favour, you must know something more about him, right? Otherwise, you wouldn't put the girls in jeopardy like that?"

"What are you talking about? What jeopardy? The guy sits at the front, having a wank while he watches the shows. So what? So do half the punters who pay the entrance fee."

Lorne's fury rose, and she could feel the heat settle in her cheeks. "What jeopardy? How can you ask that when the man ended up on the stage, groping one of the girls? A girl that just happened to go missing. You don't think that's a tad irresponsible for you to think the man's actions were entirely innocent?"

"Hey, get off my case, lady. He wasn't the only one playing up that night. Why pick on him?"

Lorne sighed heavily. "Because he's the only one I have a name for at present. I'm not picking on anyone. I'm merely trying to work through the unfortunate events of that night that might have contributed to Noelle going missing—being abducted for all we know. *Understand?*" Lorne bit her tongue for letting her impatience show at the end of her question.

"Yeah, I understand, lady. I understand you're intent on picking on this guy just because he has a few fantasies. Who said that was against the fucking law, eh?"

Lorne chewed the inside of her mouth in anger. "You're being pretty naïve if that's your interpretation of events, Mitch. Hey, a word of advice for you—never apply for a job with social services."

The other security guy laughed as Mitch's face dropped. "Ha, bloody, ha. You wanna stop flinging insults around until you get the facts you're after, lady. That would be my advice to you and your smart mouth."

Lorne smiled and winked at him. "You either give me the information you know, or I'll haul your bloody arse down the cop shop before you've had a chance to finish your OJ!"

"Yeah? Under what charge?"

"Obstructing an investigation, wasting police time, harbouring a criminal—take your pick."

Mitch pushed away from the bar, puffed out his chest, and towered over her. His colleague pulled at his arm. "Back off, Mitch. I get the impression she's the type not to mess with."

"What the hell is going on here?" Katy approached and squeezed between Lorne and her tormentor.

"This guy is teasing me with vital information to the case, Inspector," Lorne told Katy, staring the man down.

"Is that right? Then let's take this down the station and sort things out, shall we?" Katy turned her head away from the goon and winked at Lorne.

The goon's arms rose then slapped down at his sides. "Can't you tell when someone's winding you up? Jesus, someone needs to take a chill pill or something! Right, all I know is the guy lives on a nearby estate. Medway Estate, I think it's called. There, that's all I can tell you. I can do without this shit. I don't take kindly to threats, lady."

He snarled at Lorne, and she smiled back at him. "No, I hate dishing out threats in order to get information. Maybe you should consider that the next time a copper asks questions relating to a very serious case."

The music grew louder, and Lorne and Katy turned to watch Calinda take to the stage. She gyrated and bent in awkward positions around the pole to rapturous applause and cheers from the rowdy men seated around the stage. "Christ, Tony would have a heart attack if I performed like that in front of him even in the privacy of our bedroom."

Katy chuckled. "You'd probably end up in casualty after pulling a muscle in your back."

Lorne turned to look at her. "I fear you're right. What do you want to do next?"

Before Katy could answer, one of the performers swept past and motioned with her head to one of the customers: a young man in his mid-twenties, who was watching Calinda's performance rather too eagerly for Lorne's liking. "He's one of the guys," the girl said before she moved towards the other end of the bar.

Katy clutched Lorne's forearm, apparently sensing that she was about to approach the man. "Let's just watch him for a few minutes, eh?"

Lorne did as Katy requested. All the while, her stomach churned as she watched the man's head swivel this way and that while he focused intently on the dancer's gymnastic performance. As if sensing he was being watched, the man turned their way and narrowed his eyes as he assessed them. After seemingly losing interest in the entertainment, he walked briskly across the room towards the men's toilets.

"Quick, let's follow him. I'm getting the distinct impression that he's going to take off once he's out of our sight." Katy casually walked in the same direction, with Lorne close on her heels.

The man barged through the door to the men's toilets and slammed it shut in Katy's face. The lock clicked on the other side.

"Damn," Katy grumbled, kicking the base of the door.

Lorne thumbed at the exit and mouthed to Katy, "I'll go outside."

Katy knocked on the door and shouted, "Police! Open the door. We just want to ask you a few questions. There's no need for this."

Outside, Lorne darted around the side of the building. She couldn't see many options for hiding herself as she waited for the man, expecting him to attempt an escape through the toilet window. She squatted behind a bush about ten feet away. She didn't have to wait long. He dropped to the ground with a groan and scanned the area urgently, no doubt seeking an easy getaway route. Lorne left her hiding place and sprinted after him, weaving between the parked vehicles in their way. "Stop, police!"

"Screw you, lady!"

"You're only going to make things worse if you don't stop right now," Lorne called after him. The distance between them was lengthening, and her breathing had become laboured already. She knew instantly he would outrun her and she would struggle to keep up with him as he skipped over the small wall and took off up the high street. Dejected, Lorne returned to the club and went in search of Katy. She shook her head and sighed heavily. "He got away."

"Not to worry." Katy waved a disc in her hand. "The manager kept a copy of the footage from that night. Plus… I got the chance to talk to the assistant manager, who offered another name—Colin Simms."

With her heart rate nearing normal, Lorne said, "The guy who just ran off?"

"Yep."

"That's great. We can look at picking him up tomorrow, give him some breathing space. He'll think we've let him off the hook. Let's hope the disc shows us what took place that night and who the men were who jumped on the stage with Noelle. It's going to be a pain in the arse trawling through all the punters, though. Maybe someone with a previous conviction will crop up. If they've got a previous, we'll pull them in for questioning. Simms has obviously been in trouble before. Otherwise, he wouldn't have taken off like Usain Bolt."

"Okay, we've got enough to be going on with now. Let's call it a night. We've been at it for fourteen hours as it is. We'll start afresh in the morning."

Lorne puffed out her cheeks. "I'm all for that. I'm totally knackered after chasing him."

Katy dropped Lorne back at the station, where she picked up her car, and they both went their separate ways.

Entering the driveway of her home, Lorne was surprised to see that Tony's car was absent. Charlie greeted her at the back door with Henry. Lorne kissed Charlie on the cheek and bent down to cuddle her best friend, who'd been her constant companion through some very rough times in the past. "Hello, mate. How's the old legs doing?"

Henry lashed her face with kisses. Resisting the temptation to complain about his smelly breath, Lorne kissed his nose.

"He was a little tired this afternoon after his walk, Mum. I think I'll have to consider taking him for shorter walks."

Lorne ruffled the dog's head and stood up. "Well, he's getting on in years now."

"I know. Sad, really. He barely runs after his ball, either. He used to be besotted with that thing once upon a time."

"Old age catches up with us all, I suppose, at some time, Charlie. Is Tony not back yet?" Lorne closed the back door and switched on the kettle.

"Nope. He rang about twenty minutes ago, said he was on his way back. He sounded pretty pissed off, too. Don't let on that I told you. I made a chilli and saved you some, both of you."

"That's kind of you, sweetheart. I'll give it a miss tonight, if you don't mind. Katy and I ate a huge meal at lunchtime, thinking we'd be home late. I'll pop it in the freezer, unless Tony wants my share."

A car drew into the drive.

"All smiles. Let's see if we can get him out of his foul mood before it has a chance to fester," Lorne told Charlie.

The door opened, and Tony eyed them with concern. "All right, what have I done wrong?"

Lorne sauntered across the floor and slid her arms around his neck. "Is that any way to treat your adoring wife and your favourite step-daughter?"

He pecked her on the nose. "Er... that will be *only* step-daughter, unless there are other step-children of mine running around out there that I'm unaware of?"

Lorne tutted. "You've always got an answer, haven't you? How was your day?"

He buried his head into her shoulder. "Remind me why I said I wanted to become a PI again?"

Lorne pecked his cheek. "That bad, huh?"

"Our client must be nuts if he thinks his wife is cheating on him. She works endlessly long hours, end of! Joe and I have been going out of our minds all day, parked up with a set of binoculars each, and my bum..."

Lorne squeezed it with her hands, and he moaned softly.

"Well, it feels like it's been dumped in an ice pool for hours—it's that numb."

"I think I'll leave you two love birds to it. Goodnight." Rolling her eyes, Charlie mumbled under her breath as she left the room.

"You embarrassed her. How could you do that when she went out of her way to make you a meal?" Lorne pulled away and wagged a chastising finger in front of her.

"Meal? What kind of meal? A beans-on-toast variety or something far more appetizing?"

Lorne slapped his upper arm. "Has anyone ever told you how ungrateful you can be? Good job Charlie isn't around to hear you. She'd never step foot in the kitchen again. She made a chilli. Are you hungry?"

"I'm starving. Is it hot?" Tony homed in on the saucepan on top of the stove and lifted the lid. He blinked when the fumes from the pot hit him. "Yikes, it smells super hot. I'll have some if you do."

"Not unless you want a big fat momma to share your bed, hon. I've eaten one huge meal today. Couldn't face another one. Do you want rice with it? It'll take me ten minutes to cook some."

Tony took Lorne's hand and sat down at the table, pulling her onto his lap. "I'd rather have an early night and a snuggle with my adorable wife."

She pulled away from him and cocked an eyebrow. "Have you been drinking?"

"No! Can't a man be a little mushy with his wife now and again?"

"I think your job has already messed with your brain after only one day out in the field. I dread to think what you'll be like after work tomorrow night."

He nipped her neck with his teeth. "Maybe we should ask Charlie to visit her dad for a few nights."

Lorne jumped off his lap and renewed her endeavours to heat up his dinner. "Maybe you should learn to control your urges and sexual fantasies a bit more."

He placed his head in his hands and mumbled, "Spoilsport, and there was me praising what a wonderful wife I had to Joe today. Guess I'll have to reassess that and tell him the truth tomorrow."

"Shut up! Do you want to hear how my day went?" She opened the bag of rice and poured enough grains in the pot for a large helping to satisfy Tony's healthy appetite then filled the pan with boiling water from the kettle.

"Go on then. I bet it can't match mine," he jested with a smile.

"That's where you're wrong." Lorne spent the next ten minutes telling him about the cold case. By the time she got to the part about the guy absconding from the club, the food was ready to be dished up.

"Interesting case. Far better than ours, anyway. What's your gut feeling on it? Is this Noelle dead or alive?"

Lorne placed his dinner in front of him and sat down with a cup of coffee as a substitute for her own meal. "To tell you the truth, I'm not really feeling anything one way or another on this case just yet. Maybe that'll change in the coming days with the more clues or suspects that come our way. There must be something amiss for that bloke to do a runner like that."

"Yeah, or he could be some kind of druggie or something else along those lines. One whiff of a copper after him, he's sure to take off, isn't he?"

"I suppose so. I didn't get that impression, though."

Tony tentatively took a mouthful of chilli, chewed it a little, and began nodding appreciatively. "Not bad! She's obviously been watching the master at work and paying attention when I've cooked her stunning meals."

Lorne, who'd just taken a sip of coffee, spluttered the liquid across the table. "I can't believe you said that! Are you forgetting the time you put raw spaghetti in a pan on a lit stove, without water? Hmm... you men always seem to have selective memories when it suits you, don't you?"

He winked at her and took another mouthful of chilli. "I have other memories, too. Fancy an early night?"

Lorne laughed, finding it hard to resist his boyish good looks. She'd long forgotten all about the scar others saw that decorated his cheek. "Sounds like a good idea."

Tony bolted down the rest of his chilli and rinsed his plate under the tap while Lorne checked the lights to the kennels and put Henry out for his last wee of the day. Together, they climbed the stairs, arms wrapped around each other's waist with Henry at their heels. The dog turned left at the top and headed along the landing to Charlie's room.

"I think he senses he's not welcome in our room tonight," Lorne said, pushing open the door to the master bedroom. Eagerly, she dragged Tony through it then closed it behind him.

CHAPTER FOUR

The investigation began in earnest the following morning after Katy and Lorne had apprised the team of what had gone on at the club. Karen and AJ teamed up to go through the CCTV footage. They hoped two heads would prove to be better than one on that chore. Meanwhile Stephen and Graham went through the results of their house-to-house enquiries and turned up very little. A neighbour spotted a dark car in the area a few times, and that was about it.

"Great!" Katy sighed in frustration. "What is it with folks nowadays? Why can't people be more observant?"

"No sense of community, I suppose. People moving house far more often than they used to. That's my interpretation anyway." The phone on Lorne's desk rang. "Hello. DS Warner. How may I help?"

"Mum. Sorry to trouble you at work, but I think you should come home right away."

Lorne gasped then asked urgently, "Charlie? Whatever is the matter? Is it one of the dogs? Has there been an accident? Can't Tony deal with things?"

Charlie tutted. "Tony's here. It was his suggestion that I should ring you. I don't really want to go through things over the phone, Mum. Just trust me on this one, please? Oh, and you should bring Katy with you, too."

"All right, love. If you think it's that serious, we'll be there in half an hour. Can you at least give me a hint what it's concerning?"

"Carol. Can't say anything else—she won't let me."

"All right. Put the kettle on."

"What was that all about?" Katy asked, watching as Lorne replaced the phone.

"Well, knowing my lot, it's sure to be something intense. Strange that Charlie asked us both to be there."

"Let's sort the team out first then head off. I love a bit of intrigue usually. However, when it concerns your family, it always comes attached with an element of danger."

Lorne ran a hand through her hair. "Crap, don't say that. It is odd that Charlie refused to let on what it was about. I'm getting an uncomfortable feeling about this."

Ten minutes later, with the team fully instructed, Katy and Lorne swiftly made their way out of the station and into the car. Turning the key in the ignition, Katy patted Lorne on the knee with her other hand. "Stop worrying. You can be such a worry guts at times."

"Ha, with good reason, I think. Don't you? How would you react after having your daughter kidnapped and raped by my nemesis and having to deal with an 'invalid' husband thanks to the Taliban kindly taking his leg off? Not that Tony likes to be recognised as disabled. However, that's what it amounts to."

"Chill, Lorne, there's no need to snap at me. I was only winding you up. If it was anything drastic, Charlie would have sounded more panicked, wouldn't she?"

"I suppose. Just ignore me."

Fifteen minutes later, Katy pulled into Lorne's drive.

Lorne bolted out of the car and through the back door before Katy had even switched off the engine.

"What's wrong? Tell me, for goodness's sake?" Lorne's gaze took in her family and friends and eventually settled on Carol, who was sitting next to Charlie at the table, holding her hand. "Carol? What on earth is the matter? You look deathly white."

Katy burst through the kitchen, and Lorne turned to face her with wide puzzled eyes. Then she walked over to the table and sat in the seat next to Carol. She threw an arm around the woman's quivering shoulders.

"Never, never have I seen something so vivid in all my years of having this gift." Carol swallowed noisily, and Lorne's heart went out to her.

"Carol, please tell us what you've witnessed?"

The woman pulled her hand from Charlie's and covered her eyes. Then she started to rock back and forth in her chair. Lorne knew only too well what the action meant—a spirit had a hold of her and was refusing to let go until its message had been heard.

Lorne glanced up at Tony and Katy, who both looked enthralled by what was taking place. Katy stumbled across the room and sat opposite Carol.

Carol withdrew her hands and turned to stare through Katy, as if she hadn't seen her. "She was murdered."

Lorne waited a few seconds for Carol to continue before she finally asked, "Who was murdered, love?"

"The young lady reaching out to me," she said, her voice strange, sounding as if she were in a trance.

"Carol, try and get the girl's name. If she won't give it, try to get anything else she's willing to share."

Rocking back and forth again, Carol began to wail. The pitiful noise hurt Lorne's ears. "She was murdered... she roams the earth, looking for comfort... he took her life. Why?"

Out of the corner of her eye, Lorne saw Katy shudder. She smiled reassuringly at her friend. Lorne was used to Carol's behaviour—she'd witnessed it several times over the years, but this was the first time Katy had observed the psychic's abilities close up.

"Search for names, Carol. Without a name, we can't do anything, love," Lorne pleaded a second time.

Carol's head swung from side to side, and a deep guttural moan escaped her lips. Then her head dropped forward and hit the kitchen table. Lorne and Charlie helped Carol to sit upright in her chair.

"Tony, fetch me a glass of water, will you?"

Her husband also looked shocked. He jumped out of his bemused state, filled a glass sitting on the draining board, and quickly placed it before Carol.

"Drink this, sweetheart. Come back to us now." Lorne ran the rim of the glass along Carol's lip, urging her to take a sip.

Carol's hand touched Lorne's when she took the glass. "You have to help her, Lorne. Her soul will not rest, knowing that this man could do to others what he has done to her."

"We'll do everything we can to help, but we need more. You know that, love."

"I haven't slept a wink. Why me? She visited me in my bedroom last night and stayed with me throughout until the sun rose this morning. Her sobs filled my room. My heart will remain heavy while her murderer is still out there."

"I'm sorry you're going through this, sweetheart. It can't be easy to be at a spirit's beck and call in this way. Can you try asking out again? One last time?"

"I'm used to spirits visiting me, but never have I had one so determined to stay with me during the night to get their message across. Even Onyx whimpered. She wasn't scared in the slightest, but she definitely saw the spirit."

Lorne looked under the table when a head rested on her leg. "Hello, you. I didn't see you under there." Lorne encouraged the boxer out from under the table. She and Charlie had rescued and nursed the dog back to health a few months ago. "My, don't you look beautiful. Look at her coat. What a fantastic sheen." She bent down and kissed the dog's head. Onyx wriggled free and licked Lorne on the cheek.

"She's amazed everyone. Even the vet said he'd never observed such a rapid recovery from the mange."

"That's down to your love and care, Carol. She certainly landed on her feet the day you welcomed her into your home. So, Onyx sensed the spirit's presence, too?"

"Oh, yes. She's very perceptive. Most dogs are, really. People just don't realise it. Like I said, she whined and cried a little, but it was as though she was sharing the spirit's grief. It didn't freak her out at all."

"Where do we go from here, Carol?" Lorne asked, still petting the dog.

"The reason I wanted Charlie to call you out here is because I believe it must have something to do with the case you're working on."

Lorne's head snapped around. She glanced at Katy and raised a questioning eyebrow. "Shall we tell Carol the victim's name?"

Katy shrugged. "I'm not disbelieving what Carol says, but if we divulge that, wouldn't we be putting words into her mouth?"

Carol raised her hand. "I agree with Katy. Do not tell me the name. I'm sure I haven't seen the last of this spirit. When she visits next time, I'll ask her to confide in me more. Here's my line of thinking—it's too much of a coincidence not to be connected."

Lorne nodded. "You're right, totally. It has answered an important question for us, though, if we are referring to the same victim."

"What's that?" asked Katy.

"That we're looking for a corpse."

"Well, we need to rein in those thoughts for now, Lorne, until we're one hundred percent sure of the facts. If we can really deem what Carol gives us as facts. For now, I think we should keep this information between us. Am I making myself clear on that, Tony? Charlie?"

Everyone agreed.

Lorne kissed Carol on the cheek. "How are you feeling now?"

"I'll be fine. You know how it is with me. Once the information has flowed from my lips, I feel a thousand times better, until the next episode."

"Listen, why don't you go home? Try and catch up on your sleep. I'm sure Charlie can cope around here today. Can't you, love?"

"Of course I can. You'll help if I need you, won't you, Tony?"

Tony nodded and filled the kettle. "This morning, I can. I need to get back to my surveillance duties this afternoon."

"Then that's sorted. You go home and rest. Perhaps the spirit will try to contact you again if you're at home in a relaxed environment." Lorne smiled at Carol.

"All right. You've beaten me into submission. Let me have a nice cup of coffee first, and then Onyx and I will toddle off home. How are things going with the case you're working on? No names, remember?"

Lorne sniggered. "Frustrating the hell out of us right now. We could certainly use your help. We're at a kind of crossroads until more information falls into our laps."

"Yeah, ain't that the truth? Same here, Tony. We'll have a drink then get off, if you don't mind." Katy issued a toothy grin in his direction.

"Back to tea and coffee boy, am I?"

Lorne left the table, hooked her arms around his waist, and rested her head on his back. "You know you're appreciated."

"When it suits," he grumbled good-naturedly.

Carol, Lorne, and Katy all left the premises at the same time, but in two separate cars.

"Well, that was the oddest thirty minutes I've spent in your family's company for a while," Katy stated as she pulled into the flow of traffic on the road that led back to the station.

"I just wish we could have informed Carol of the victim's name. Maybe it would have prompted her—or the spirit, if it was there listening in on our conversation—to offer up some vital information to help us crack the case."

Katy tutted. "I don't know, Lorne. Let's tamper down our excitement over this revelation for the time being, eh? I'd rather do that than end up with some of that yellow-coloured stuff that comes out of a chicken's bum on my face, especially as this case is already under a vast amount of scrutiny from our superiors. Before you object—I believe Carol. I truly do. We just need to be cautious with this one. Agreed?"

"Yep, I suppose you're right. One question for you, though."

"Go for it," Katy said, glancing sideways at her.

"Do eggs really come out of a chicken's backside?"

They both roared with laughter at her bizarre observation.

At the station, Katy buried herself in paperwork in her office for the next few hours while Lorne organised the team. In spite of her unexpected visit back home and the hour they had wasted, the morning proved to be very productive.

Karen and AJ continued to search through the CCTV discs, on the lookout for guys entering the club alone. As midday approached, AJ called Lorne over.

"What have you found, AJ?" She perched her rear on the nearest desk and leaned forward to view his computer screen, which showed four individual frames.

"We came up with four possible suspects. The rest of the clientele arrived in groups, so we discounted them immediately." Each frame showed a man entering the club.

"It's a start. We might need to revisit that later if the suspects prove to be a waste of time. However, the security guys didn't let on that the men who jumped on the stage that night were in a group." Lorne pointed at the frame in the top-right corner. "That's Simms, the guy I chased in the car park. Karen, did you find out anything when you brought up his details earlier?"

"Yep, I'll get the results." Karen wheeled her chair across the floor to her own desk to retrieve the information while Lorne and AJ continued with the search.

"Okay. Can we look at each individual and how they react when they enter the club? I'm looking for one of the men to show some form of agitation. The security bod thought he might be a little simple."

"I don't need to look back." AJ pointed at one of the men on the bottom row. "He looked mighty shifty when he walked into the place. He seemed pretty friendly with the bouncer though, which puzzled me."

"In what way?"

"His reactions were just odd. If he was known to the bouncer, then why would he exude some discomfort?"

"Then that's the Gary the security guard inside was talking about." Lorne pulled out the notebook from her jacket pocket. "He even gave me a possible address for this Gary. Unfortunately, he couldn't supply a surname for him."

"Well, he should be easy enough to track down. Do you want me to print off a picture?"

"Sure. Print off all four. At last, we seem to be getting somewhere."

Katy joined them, and Lorne relayed what they had managed to find out in her absence.

"Great, if we can pull some names and addresses, we could get out there and interview these people, at least a few of them this afternoon, Lorne."

The phone on Karen's desk rang. She answered it then waved an excited arm to get their attention before she hung up. "That was the BBC. They've had to pull one of the stories they were running and wanted to let us know that the reconstruction is going to be filmed this afternoon and be shown on tomorrow's *Crimewatch*."

Katy clapped her hands together. "Wow, great timing. Karen, can you oversee the reconstruction for me?"

"I'd love to. Here's some more good news for you, boss." Karen withdrew the sheet of paper from her printer tray and gave it to Katy. "Colin Simms. He's a mechanic. Owns a garage not far from the club, just around the corner, in fact."

"Interesting. Good job, Karen. Let's hope we get a matching positive result from the reconstruction. Do your best for me."

"Leave it with me, boss."

"Want to set off now or after lunch?" Lorne asked, standing alongside Katy.

"Let's go now. Strike before anyone gets the notion we're on to them."

Lorne snorted. "I have a feeling that Simms already has that impression, don't you?"

"Smartarse! What else have we got?"

AJ glanced up. "We just need to try and find a name for these two now." He waved a hand at the computer screen.

"Has everyone on the team seen the pics, AJ?"

He shook his head. "Steve and Graham, come over here and take a gander at these two."

Lorne and Katy stepped back, allowing the two men access to the screen.

Stephen bent down to take a closer look while AJ zoomed in on the two unnamed suspects. "No idea."

Graham clicked his fingers then pointed to the man wearing a bomber jacket. "Now that one I do recognise." He scratched the top of his head and squeezed his eyes shut as he wracked his brain. "Can you give me half an hour? Something at the back of my mind is leaning towards a convicted sex offender, maybe a minor charge, but still an offender, all the same."

"Shoo… do what you have to do to come up with the name, Graham," Katy ordered him back to his desk to start his search.

"Sounds promising," Lorne said, nudging Katy's elbow.

"Let's delay our little excursion until Graham gets back to us. We might as well visit all the men this afternoon. If we get the chance, are you up for that?"

"Yep, suits me."

"Eureka!" Graham shouted. "Chris Dilbert. I had the initials CD going through my head, just couldn't remember his name. I seem to recall a case where he assaulted two schoolgirls in a park close to my home about eighteen months ago. He was banged up for the offence but released earlier this year. Here's his address, boss."

"Smashing. Great teamwork, guys. Let's hope all this information leads us to Noelle's probable killer," Katy called out triumphantly.

"Killer?"

Lorne spun around to find Diana Chesterfield standing in the doorway with the station's desk sergeant. *Shit! I'm glad I'm not filling Katy's shoes right now.*

Katy walked towards the woman and placed a hand on her arm. "I'm sorry, Mrs. Chesterfield. I didn't see you there." She turned to the desk sergeant and issued a tight-lipped smile, letting him know how ticked off she was at the unannounced visit.

"You said killer. Is Noelle dead, Inspector?"

"Let's take this into my office. I'll bring you up to date on the case. Thank you, Sergeant. You can get back to your post now."

The sergeant's shoulders slumped, and he turned to leave the incident room.

Katy asked Mrs. Chesterfield to follow her and tapped Lorne on the shoulder as she passed. "Will you join us, too, Sergeant Warner?"

"Of course. Would you like a drink, Mrs. Chesterfield?"

"No, thank you. All I need is information," she replied abruptly.

Once they were all seated, Katy intertwined her fingers and placed her hands on the desk. "We've obtained most of our pertinent information just this morning, over the past few hours. The sergeant and I haven't had the chance to even interview any of the people we suspect have a possible connection to your daughter's case. I have not deliberately kept you out of the loop, I assure you."

"Really, Inspector? Then what's all this nonsense about a killer? Have you found my… baby's body?"

"No, we haven't."

Mrs. Chesterfield let out a heavy sigh. "Then pray tell me what you are referring to? I think I have a right to know, don't you?"

"Yes, of course you do. Right now, we've uncovered leads, not concrete evidence. For all we know, what we've learnt could be totally false or have nothing to do with Noelle or her disappearance. You wouldn't forgive me, us, for giving you misinformation."

"I suppose so. Can I ask what type of *leads* you do have?"

"At the moment, all we're aware of is that there were a couple of problems Noelle had during her last stint at the club."

"Problems? What kind of problems would lead you to suspect Noelle is… no longer with us?"

"Three men, umm… disrupted your daughter's dance that evening. Of course, those men will be where our investigation begins. Please, I'm begging you to bear with us for a little while longer. I know you feel the Met has let you down in the past, rightly so, but my partner and I are doing everything we can to right the wrongs that have gone before us."

"So, why are you hanging around here and not out there tracking down these suspects?"

"You have every right to ask that question. I must reiterate that this information has only just come our way—in fact, we're still collating it. Once we have everything to hand, then we will be out there, searching for the suspects and pulling them in for questioning."

"Very well. Have you found my daughter's car yet?" Mrs. Chesterfield asked, nodding her head in satisfaction at Katy's explanation.

"Not yet. There is something I was going to call you about."

"And what's that, Inspector?" The woman sat forward in her seat.

"That the BBC programme *Crimewatch* will be running a reconstruction in their show planned to air this week."

"Marvellous news. Why wasn't that carried out when Noelle first went missing?" She waved a dismissive hand. "No need to answer that. Those idiots couldn't organise their own grandmothers' funerals," she stated with a curled lip.

"We'll keep you up to date with what comes our way from the show. Maybe it would be better if you didn't watch the show."

"I'll take your advice on board."

"Is there anything else we can help you with?"

"No. Forgive my abruptness, won't you, Inspector. It's the being left in the dark that is hard to take, knowing that somewhere, someone knows what happened to my daughter. How can people live with themselves? It really is beyond me. And if ever I lay eyes on the two morons who supposedly investigated the case the first time around... well, I just hope you're there to witness it, because you'll need to restrain me from taking my frustrations out on their heads with a cricket bat."

"Let's hope you never meet them in that case. I'd hate for you to get into trouble over those two officers. My partner and I will bring your daughter's case to a conclusion, whether it has a happy ending or not."

Mrs. Chesterfield stood and extended her hand across the table.

Katy rose from her chair and clasped the woman's hand in both of hers. "Give us a little more time."

"I will. But, in return, please don't hide any details from me. I know the odds are stacked against us for finding Noelle alive. However, I *need* to be able to cling on to the faintest hope that she's out there, praying that we'll find her."

"I understand. You have my guarantee that I'll keep you informed of our progress, Mrs. Chesterfield. I'll ring you on Friday with an update, how's that?"

"You're very kind, Inspector."

Katy led the woman to the station's exit.

In the incident room, Lorne slumped into her chair and placed her head in her hands. "Crap, that could have been far worse. Katy handled her remarkably well. That poor woman must be sitting at home, climbing the walls for news, and to come here and hear us acknowledge that she could have been killed must have been a real shock to her system."

"Poor woman." Karen shook her head. "I dread to think how I'd react under the same circumstances. Sod Travers and Campbell for trashing innocent peoples' lives like this."

"The thing is, Karen, as a team, we've accomplished far more in one morning than those dickheads managed in two months. What utter jerks they were—are. Let's hope they get banged up and someone misplaces the key for bloody years to come. And don't forget, this is only one case they've royally fucked up! There are dozens more people out there in the same position as Mrs. Chesterfield."

Katy entered the incident room again near the end of Lorne's speech. "Well, I've just assured Mrs. Chesterfield that we will conclude this case by the end of next week. I know I shouldn't have said it, but, by Christ, I'm going to go the extra mile to ensure that frigging happens. Who's with me?"

The team roared and raised their hands. "Too right!" AJ shouted, speaking for the rest of the team.

CHAPTER FIVE

"I think we should split up," Lorne said as Katy stopped the vehicle on the edge of the industrial estate.

"I'll go in the front while you take up a position around the back, in case Simms tries to do a runner again," Katy said.

"I'll hop out here." Lorne jumped out of the car and walked casually around the rear of the three buildings leading up to the car mechanic's workshop owned by Colin Simms. She pressed herself against the metal façade of the building next to the back door and waited.

She heard shouting in the distance, followed by a loud crash, which sounded like tools hitting a solid floor. Katy ordered the man to stop.

Lorne inhaled a large breath, her hands clenched anxiously at her sides. Suddenly, the door flew open. Simms looked as shocked to see her as she was to see him. "Stop right there, Simms," she ordered.

"Fuck off!" he growled and took a swipe at her with a huge monkey wrench.

Lorne ducked, avoiding the heavy tool before it made contact with her face. The man sprinted, his speed increasing with every long stride of his athletic legs. A little dazed, Lorne took off in pursuit.

"Shit, Lorne, why didn't you stop him?" Katy chastised as she flew out of the door and bolted after him.

"I tried," Lorne shouted.

"It doesn't matter now. We have to get him before he manages to get away—again."

Two workmen walked out of one of the other buildings and cast confused glances their way.

"Police! Stop that man," Katy shouted.

The two men stood in Simms's path and tried to wrestle with him, but he easily pushed the men aside.

"Shit!" Katy hissed.

A sinking feeling settled in Lorne's stomach as the absconder jumped into his car and screeched out of the car park.

Katy bent over and placed her hands on her knees. Lorne jogged up beside her and placed a hand on her back. In between breaths, she tried to apologise. "Sorry, Katy. He caught me off-guard, tried to clobber me with that wrench."

"Not to worry. If those two guys couldn't stop him, I doubt we would've been able to prevent his getaway. I'll get in touch with the station, ask them to keep an eye out for his car. He can't hide forever."

"That's true. Was there any other members of staff inside the workshop?" Lorne asked, still gasping for breath during her sentence.

"No. So he would need to return here today to secure the place—is that what you're thinking?"

"Yep, there's an awful lot of valuable kit lying around in a mechanic's garage. My ex, Tom, used to be one, so I should know. Why don't we get a surveillance team out here to wait for him to return?"

"I'll ring the station and get that organised. I suppose he might ask a friend to drop by to secure the place for him."

"Well, if he does that, we can pull the guy in for aiding and abetting. He's sure to let slip where Simms is hiding out rather than take the flack himself."

Katy turned her back and placed the call to put the plan into action. Meanwhile, Lorne took down the two men's names and addresses and asked if they would be willing to give a statement about what had taken place. Then they walked back to the car and drove to the next interviewee's house on their list.

Medway Estate was comprised of what looked to be council starter homes erected about thirty to forty years ago. Some of the properties were in better repair than others.

"There's a car parked in this driveway. Let's knock on the door and show them Gary's picture," Katy said, leaving the vehicle. They walked up the cracked concrete path beside the car, and Katy rang the bell.

The door, tethered to the jamb by a chain, opened a crack. "Hello?" a woman called.

"Sorry to trouble you. We're looking for this young man." Katy shoved the photo through the crack, and the woman took it. "We know he lives in this area. We're just not sure of his address."

"I know him. Why do you want him? Who are you?"

Katy winced and put her ID through the doorway. "I apologise, I should have shown you my warrant card before asking about Gary."

"That's okay, dear. You can't be too careful nowadays, can you? Let me take this chain off. Hold on a minute."

The woman opened the door and smiled at them. "Gary James lives in the house opposite with his mum, Maureen. I do hope he's not in any kind of trouble. He has a heart of gold, that boy. He's just misunderstood by people who don't know him."

"That's brilliant. Thank you for the character reference. That's a great help. Sorry to bother you." Katy retrieved the picture from the woman, and they headed across the road to knock on the Jameses door.

"Well, that turned out to be far easier than anticipated," Lorne stated, turning to survey the residential area.

"Let's hope our good luck continues once we're inside."

A woman wearing an apron opened the door. Flour decorated the tip of her nose and half of her right cheek. "Yes?"

"Mrs. James? I'm DI Katy Foster, and this is my partner DS Lorne Warner. We're from the Met. Would it be all right if we came in for a chat?"

"Chat about what? What have I done wrong? If it's about that tiff I had with that shop assistant, we sorted it out there and then."

"No, it's nothing like that. Please, it would be better if we talked inside," Katy insisted.

The woman held open the door, allowing them to enter the house, and closed it behind them. "Go through to the living room. You'll have to excuse the mess. I like to do my baking just after lunch before I do my other chores. I'm out cleaning offices first thing in the morning. Must stick to my routine, or things have a tendency to go awry and I end up accomplishing nothing."

They walked into the room to find the young man they had come to see, sitting in his pyjamas, watching daytime TV.

"Gary, turn that bloody thing off. Can't you see we have guests? And go and put some flipping clothes on."

Gary hit the standby button then threw the control on the sofa next to him. His arms crossed sternly in objection, he bowed his head until it rested on his chest, his eyes sneaking a look at Lorne and Katy.

"It's okay, Mrs. James. We're actually here to see Gary."

"What? Why?" Mrs. James asked nervously.

"Can we all sit down and talk about this calmly?" Katy said, offering the woman a reassuring smile.

"Of course. Let me turn off the oven, and I'll be right with you. Gary, go and get your dressing gown on at least."

"He's fine," Lorne assured the woman before she scurried out of the room.

Mrs. James returned a few seconds later and sat in one of the easy chairs, her hands fretfully playing with her apron in her lap. Her gaze darted between the other three persons present in the room. "Okay, what's this about? Gary is ill. Anything he might have done wrong might be attributed to his illness."

Gary scowled at his mother. "Mum! I ain't ill. I ain't done nothin' wrong."

"At the moment, we're just making enquiries, Mrs. James." Katy turned her attention to Gary while Lorne took her notebook from her pocket in readiness. "Gary, do you work?"

"Yes." He buried his head deeper into his chest to avoid eye contact with the detectives and his distressed mother.

"It's his day off today, hence his laziness. He's a good boy. Why are you here, detectives?" Gary's mother pleaded.

"Where do you work, Gary?" Katy continued, ignoring his mother.

Mrs. James wriggled out of her chair and stood in the middle of the room with her hands digging into her sides. "I asked a question of my own. Gary, don't answer her question."

"It's all right, Mum. Chill out."

"Detectives?" her voice boomed and reverberated around the small space.

"There's no need to get irate, Mrs. James. Please be patient," Katy responded, her own tone riddled with frustration.

"Then get to your point, Inspector. Why do you want to know where Gary works?"

"I'm trying to get some background information about your son. Okay, here's the thing—please take a seat. I don't think you're going to like what I have to say."

Mrs. James threw herself into the worn-out easy chair again and stared expectantly at Katy. "Go on."

Katy revealed why they were there. All the time, her gaze remained glued to Gary, gauging his reactions. "How often do you visit the Tickle Club, Gary?"

"What? He doesn't go there! Do you, love?" Mrs. James interrupted. Her face dropped when her son refused to deny the claim.

"I'm afraid your son quite often frequents the club. Don't you, Gary?"

The young man raised his head a little and raked a hand through his hair. "I… umm… sometimes go there."

"You *don't*. Oh my! How could you?"

"Mrs. James, please try and remain calm. Otherwise, I will have to ask you to either leave the room or insist on Gary accompanying us to the station to answer our questions. What's it to be?"

The woman reluctantly nodded and sat back in her chair. She stared at her son through narrowed eyes as Katy continued to question him.

"How often, Gary?"

"Once or twice a week—when I can get out, that is."

Lorne cringed when she heard his mother tut. She knew how disgusted the woman was with the revelation that her sweet, innocent son preferred to venture into the seedier parts of the town rather than spend the evening at home with her. Thankfully, Mrs. James suppressed her anger.

"How can you afford the entrance fee?"

"Rob on the door lets me in for free most of the time. Is that wrong? Is that why you're here to arrest me, for getting in there free?"

Katy smiled at the frowning young man. "No, we're not here to arrest you for anything, Gary. We're here to try and piece a puzzle together. That's all."

"Oh! I see. I like puzzles." He pointed at a shelf stacked high with boxes. "I do them all the time. Don't I, Mum?"

"Huh! Yes, when you're not going to indecent places like that club. Oh, son! How could you?" his mother's voice rose a few octaves.

"It's fun, Mum. Lots of men go, even a few women sometimes," he replied with all the innocence of a teenage boy.

Katy interrupted their conversation with another pertinent question. "Gary, I need you to cast your mind back about six months ago."

"I'll try my hardest."

"We have this picture of you at the Tickle Club the night Noelle Chesterfield was dancing. Do you remember Noelle, Gary?"

His cheeks flushed a crimson colour. "Yes. I haven't seen her lately. She's lovely."

The way he said the words made Lorne shudder inside. The guy seemed innocent enough, but when someone with his subdued mental capacity was confronted with a girl wiggling her bits, who's to say how he should react?

"Well, still casting your mind back, can you tell us about that night? The last night you saw Noelle at the club?"

His brow furrowed, his mouth moved from side to side as he thought, and he scratched his temple. Lorne noticed that his hand was shaking.

Well, that isn't a good sign.

"Gary? Do you need me to refresh your memory some more?" Katy asked, her gaze widening as she glanced at Lorne then back at the suspect.

His mouth remained tightly shut until his mother's voice broke him out of his reverie. "Do as the detectives say, Gary, or I'll ban you from watching the TV for a month."

At the thought of losing such a privilege, the incensed young man glared at his mother as if she'd just risen up from hell itself to punish him.

"All I know is there was trouble that night," Gary eventually admitted.

"Go on," Katy prompted, issuing Mrs. James with a grateful smile.

"One man jumped up on stage to talk to Noelle. I watched him. Noelle screamed, and the staff grabbed him. Threw him out of the club."

"What happened next, Gary?"

"Then another man climbed onto the stage…"

"And, Gary? Is that when you took your chance to get on the stage, too?" Katy asked calmly.

Silence filled the room for an instant. Then Gary shot out of his chair and began pacing the worn-out carpet in front of them, his trembling hand running through his greasy hair. "I didn't mean to do it. I wanted to say hello to Noelle. That's all."

"But you ended up scaring her. Is that right?" Katy asked.

Lorne's gaze drifted from her partner, to Gary, then his mother. She had a feeling things were going to become tricky and the young man was about to take flight. This time, she would ensure the suspect didn't get away, not that he'd probably get very far in his pyjamas anyway.

His mother opened her mouth to chastise Gary again, although a warning glance from Katy put paid to that idea.

"Answer me, Gary. You're not in any trouble. We just need to hear the truth, the facts about what took place that evening. Can you enlighten us? Fill in some of the gaps, please?" Katy corrected herself.

This statement only seemed to make Gary even more agitated. He upped his pace and began tugging at clumps of his hair with clenched hands, a pained expression pulling at his face.

"She smiled at me... I wanted to kiss her... to touch..." Gary paused and searched out his mother, possibly seeking her forgiveness.

Mrs. James's hand covered her cheek. "What are you saying, Gary? Did you attack that girl? Detectives, please tell me what this is all about. I don't think my son should say anything else without a solicitor being present."

Katy raised a hand. "We're not accusing Gary of anything, Mrs. James. At the moment, we're simply following up on a lead in this case. It's entirely up to you if you'd like to take this down the station and call in the services of a brief."

"No! I don't want to go to the station. I've done nothing wrong," Gary pleaded, fear resonating in his voice as the tears welled up in his terrified eyes.

"Then tell us what happened," Katy urged with a coaxing smile.

"Nothing. As soon as she screamed, I ran, jumped off the stage. I didn't want to hurt nobody."

"What about the other man?" Lorne asked before Katy could ask the same question.

"He stayed up there with her. He had his hands all over her. I wanted to pull him off..."

"Why didn't you, Gary?" Katy asked quietly.

"I was confused. The shouting... I couldn't think straight... he was bigger than me." He looked in his mother's direction and shrugged. "I forgot to take my medication that day. I was excited and forgot it."

His mother inhaled and let out a long shuddering breath. She reached out her hand. Gary walked hesitantly towards her and knelt. Mrs. James cradled her son and rocked him back and forth, his head resting on her large breasts. "There, there, love. Everything will turn out all right."

Lorne was of two minds whether to cringe at the obvious mother-son bond or feel sorry for the young man and his mum for living with his condition daily. By the looks of things, Gary regularly needed a comforting and a guiding hand to cling to.

"Gary, I can see how upset you are. Don't give up now. Try to answer our questions honestly," Katy said.

He sat back on his heels and stared at Katy. "I am answering them honestly. I've told you all what went on. I swear I have."

"Okay. What happened when you left the stage? Did you go back to your seat?"

He shook his head and cast his eyes down to the floor. "No. I left the club."

Lorne and Katy exchanged worried glances. "Can you recall what time that was, Gary?"

He pondered a while then said, "About eleven, I guess."

"When you left the club, did you come straight home?"

He nodded and said abruptly, "Yes."

"Can anyone back that up?" Katy asked.

"I don't think so. Mum was in bed. She always goes to bed at ten. I try not to wake her if I go out and come home late."

"I'm always awake, listening out for him, though," Mrs. James added, quickly jumping to his defence.

"There's a problem with that as you probably won't be able to remember what occurred the night in question," Katy pointed out.

"Agreed. Detectives, I will say one thing—Gary might be ill, but he's not a liar. Telling lies would destroy all the hard work the doctors have put in to his treatment over the years. You can check with the specialist at the hospital if you don't believe me. They run yearly tests to ensure nothing has changed within his brain. He has good days, mostly good, and bad days, those are the killers. He throws a bigger strop than a two-year-old child. It's his escape mechanism, his way of getting it out of his system. If he didn't vent his feelings, he'd go downhill rapidly. Like I said, Gary isn't a liar. He might be guilty of being misled at times, but can never be deemed a liar."

"Thank you, Mrs. James. That helps us to understand a lot. The thing is, we have to ask these questions of your son because the next day, Noelle had a problem with an intruder at her flat. When she left the flat to drive to a friend's house, she vanished. The young lady hasn't been seen or heard from since that day."

"Oh Lord, I had no idea," Mrs. James said, eyeing her son with suspicion. "Gary? Look at me. Gary?"

Her son's head turned in slow motion to face her. "Mum, I don't know anything about this, I promise you." He wiped away a tear dangling from his long lashes.

Mrs. James nodded. "Then that's good enough for me. Detectives, no one knows my son better than I do. Not the doctors prescribing his damn tablets. No one. He's not, and never will be, a liar."

Katy stood, and Lorne copied her partner.

Extending her hand, Katy told the woman, "Then that's good enough for us. One final thing before we leave, if I may?" She approached Gary and touched his arm. "Gary, if you hear anything about Noelle, will you promise to tell your mum?" The distraught man nodded. "And if that happens, Mrs. James, will you give me a call right away?" Katy handed the woman one of her business cards.

"You have my word on that, Inspector. I hope you find this poor girl, and soon."

In the car, Lorne turned to Katy. "What's your take on the lad?"

Katy leaned back against the headrest. "I'm not sure. Maybe we should keep him in mind as a distant suspect. I've got differing feelings about him right now. What about you?"

"I'm thinking along the same lines. There's no way that lad should be visiting a place like the Tickle Club. Even if he's not guilty of doing something to Noelle, someone with his disposition could easily end up carrying out a sexual assault only because they don't really know what's right and what's wrong. I'm not tarring all people with learning difficulties with the same brush, but really, introducing them to something that could incite such strong emotions or desires of a sexual nature seems a dangerous mix. Sorry, that's just my point of view on the matter."

Katy glanced her way. "I'm with you one thousand percent…" Katy's mobile rang. "Yes… that's great. Slap some cuffs on him. We'll shoot over there now." She hung up and started the engine.

"Simms has turned up at his workshop. Let's see what he has to say for himself, shall we?"

CHAPTER SIX

Colin Simms was incensed when they returned to the mechanic's workshop. The look on his face reminded Lorne of a wounded bull ready to defend his last ounce of blood.

Katy and Lorne walked up to the man, who the two uniformed police at the scene had restrained in handcuffs that attached him to a metal workbench off to one side of the garage. "Mr. Simms, glad to make your acquaintance at last. I'm DI Katy Foster, and this is my partner, DS Lorne Warner."

"What am I supposed to have done wrong? You can't just come in here and slap these things on me, for shit's sake." He rattled the cuffs against the bench, and the noise of metal hitting metal circulated the area.

"For a start, you ran from us. To us, that's a good indication that you have something to hide. What is that, Mr. Simms?"

His gaze dropped to the concrete floor, and he shuffled his feet. Embarrassment chased away the rage from his features, but he refused to speak.

Katy took a step closer to the suspect. "Mr. Simms? You're only going to make matters worse for yourself if you clam up."

Still, the man refused to talk. Lorne could tell he was busy thinking carefully about his predicament, presumably telling himself how foolish it would be to open his mouth and drop himself in the mire. "This is obviously going to waste more of our valuable time, Inspector. I think we should head back to the station and place Mr. Simms under caution. We've got a heavy day ahead of us. Not sure we'll be able to squeeze in an interview today, though."

"Hmm… you're right, Sergeant." Katy clicked her fingers, playing along with Lorne's suggestion. "We might have a spare hour first thing in the morning, I suppose. Of course, anything could happen in between now and then. You know the nick's reputation for dodgy food and sharing cells with criminals yet to have their sanity assessed by the police surgeon, but he should be all right. We'll just have to take that risk, won't we?"

Lorne tutted and shook her head. "Never thought of that side of things, Inspector." Out of the corner of her eye, she watched Simms's head swivel rapidly between the two detectives.

"I'm not sitting in any cell overnight. I'm telling you, I've done nothing wrong."

"If that's right, then why have you run away from us twice in the last twenty-four hours?"

"Because... well, it's not every day you coppers come looking for me."

"Is there supposed to be some form of logic to your reply buried in that observation, Mr. Simms?"

"I've had some mates lose their businesses because of you guys snooping around and causing hassle."

"Okay, let's get one thing straight. That's bullshit, and you damn well know it. For a start, we first laid eyes on you at the club. That had nothing to do with your business. Am I correct?" Katy asked, raising a questioning eyebrow as she folded her arms.

"I... um..."

"Yes, Mr. Simms? You can see where I'm leading here, can't you?" Katy continued, impatiently tapping her foot.

"All right, you've got me on that one. What's this all about then?"

"One of the dancers at the club," Katy told him.

"Which one? I'm not sure what any dancer has to do with me. I'm still confused, and these cuffs are only adding to my confusion." He clanged the offending items against the bench again to emphasise his point.

"Tough. Why should we trust you after you've given us the slip several times already? Anyway, as I was saying, the dancer is called Noelle."

His eyes widened in recognition.

"The same dancer you climbed on the stage with about six months ago. Don't tell me you can't remember that incident?"

He shrugged his right shoulder. "I remember it, and I also regretted it the instant I did it. Oh, and just for your information, I wasn't the only one to hop up on the stage that night. Two other guys took the plunge to chance their arms, too."

"So, what you're saying is that men are like sheep. You see one person do something, and you perceive it as though you're missing out in some way. Is that right?"

"No!"

"Then tell me, enlighten me what goes on in that warped mind of yours. You knew the club's rules about confronting the dancers."

"Yeah, I know the rules. Look, if you must know, I took the chance to try and get to know her while the security guys were busy escorting that other guy off the premises. I liked Noelle, thought we could be good together, and wanted to ask her out."

Katy and Lorne shared an incredulous look. "Make a habit of picking up dancing girls, girls who reveal their wares to a wide audience, Mr. Simms, do you?"

"No! Jesus, she was different. Anyone could see that just by watching her. She doesn't like doing that job—any idiot can see that. She *has* to do it to get her through university."

Katy tilted her head. "You seem to know an awful lot about this young lady. How come?"

"I've already told you, she was one of the friendlier girls. I chatted to her at the bar a few nights before. Nothing wrong in that, is there?"

"Nothing at all, ordinarily."

"What's that supposed to effing mean?" he demanded quickly, frowning.

Lorne could tell his anger was mounting again. Maybe he sensed that he was getting backed into a corner.

Katy glanced at Lorne. "Do you think we should tell him, Sergeant?"

Lorne nodded and looked up at the clock on the wall. It was almost four. "I think we should. Time's getting on, Inspector."

"You're right. Okay, Mr. Simms, here's the thing. After you *confronted* Noelle Chesterfield at her place of work, the very next day, the young lady in question had an intruder in her flat."

"No way are you gonna pin that on me, lady. I ain't no friggin' perv."

Katy raised a hand to silence him. "But that was only the beginning of the story, Mr. Simms. Not long after the incident occurred, Noelle went missing."

"Along with her car," Lorne added.

"What? I haven't done anything wrong. You can't lay this at my bloody door. You hear me? I'll get the best solicitor I can find."

"That's your entitlement. I will point out something, though," Katy warned. "You better tell your brief that in the past few days, you've avoided talking to us. Even he will think that's a strange thing for an innocent man to do. Agreed?"

"Shit, all right. All right, here's the deal. I'll tell you the real reason I ran off, and it's got nothing to do with this missing girl. I swear." Simms paused and glanced around at all four members of the police standing in his workshop. "Jesus, I clock vehicles and issue dodgy MOTs."

"What? And that's why you ran? Seriously?" Katy asked, running a hand through her hair. "You mean we've wasted bloody hours of our valuable time trying to track you down, and this is why you took a hike?"

"Yeah. I swear I have nothing to do with Noelle's disappearance. I just wouldn't do that to her or any other girl."

Katy exhaled noisily. "You'll forgive me if I find that hard to believe given the line of underhand business you're in and the fact that you jumped up on stage to confront the young lady, won't you, Simms?"

Lorne pulled Katy aside before Simms could reply. "We're going to have to take him in, after what he's just admitted. My instinct is that he doesn't know anything about Noelle's attack, either directly or indirectly. He appeared too shocked when you gave him the information, for one thing."

"You're right. Let's wrap this up and see if we can track this other bloke down—Dilbert, wasn't it?"

Lorne gave a brief nod. "That's what I'd do. Let the uniformed guys take Simms back to the station and deal with him."

Katy turned and eyed the suspect with distaste then pointed at him. "This is your lucky day, kind of. We're up against time on this case, so this is what's going to happen. Our colleagues here are going to take you down the station, where you'll tell an interviewing officer what exactly you've been up to here. Names, dates, the type of money involved in this scam. If you don't cooperate, then we'll have no hesitation in pinning Noelle's disappearance on you. Got that? After all, you fancied the pants off her, excuse the pun, and that amounts to motive when someone is reported missing."

Simms's mouth hung open for several seconds.

Then Katy prompted him for a response. "Do I make myself clear on this, Mr. Simms?"

"Yes. I'm willing to divulge contacts, *et cetera*, but please, scrub me off the wanted list for Noelle's case. I'd never hurt her, ever. I promise."

"It depends how cooperative you are. Okay, guys, take him back and caution him."

"What about this place? I need to lock up first," Simms whined.

"Funny that, you weren't too bothered about locking up earlier. Why should now be any different?" Katy asked.

"Please, I've said I'm sorry. I can't leave this place unattended. There's too much kit here to leave it open to all and sundry to rob."

"All right. You have five minutes to secure the place. Uncuff him, lads. Lorne and I will stick around in case he tries to bolt again."

The two uniformed officers temporarily freed the suspect from the cuffs and stuck with him like adhesive until the garage had been thoroughly secured.

Outside, with the cuffed suspect placed in the back of the vehicle, they watched the Panda car drive off before getting in their own car and heading off for the next location. "Let's hope this Dilbert fella is at home."

Lorne snapped her seatbelt into place. "My money is on him being either at work or out."

"What's with the negative attitude all of a sudden?" Katy asked, selecting first gear and driving out of the estate.

"I'm not negative. Just stating facts. After what else we've had to contend with today, I doubt things are going to start going our way now."

"We'll see in about twenty minutes. If he's not there, we'll head back to the station and call it a day. All right?"

The heavy traffic delayed them getting to Dilbert's address, and when they knocked on the door of the shabby-looking terrace, there was no reply. Lorne and Katy nipped next door and asked the neighbours a few questions about his comings and goings, but no one could tell them anything specific. In the end, they agreed it would be best to leave it for the day and return to try again the following day, providing nothing urgent showed up to distract them in the meantime.

* * *

Lorne opened the back door to her house and called out to see if anyone was at home. "I'm back. Where are you all?" She heard running on the stairs, then Charlie came through the door with an out-of-breath Henry at her heels.

"Hi, Mum. Did you have a good day?"

"Not really. What about you, sweetie? Have you heard from Carol since she left earlier?"

Charlie sat at the kitchen table and clicked her fingers to get the dog's attention. "No, I was going to ring her and then thought better of it. Maybe we should leave her for today, let her catch up on her sleep. I can't imagine what it must be like sitting up all night, having a conversation with a spook."

Lorne placed two cups of coffee on the table and dropped heavily into the chair opposite her daughter. "I can't imagine and *never* want to ever experience anything like that, either. Saying that, on the odd occasion when I've felt Pete and your granddad around me, it has turned out to be a great source of comfort."

"Yeah, I can understand that, but a tortured soul such as this Noelle would definitely put the willies up me." Charlie shuddered.

"Has Tony rung?"

"Nope. What shall we have for dinner? Want me to help you prepare it?"

"Crap, I haven't really given it much thought, love. It's been a super-hectic kind of day today."

"Let's have a makeshift meal then. What about those lovely filled jacket spuds you do? I'll chop a few veggies while you sort out the potatoes, if you like."

"Good idea. Let me have this first, eh?" Lorne savoured the first hot cup of coffee that had passed her lips all day and sighed contentedly. She groaned when the phone in the lounge started ringing.

"Stop. I'll get it, Mum." Charlie ran into the lounge and returned with the phone. "See you later. Here's Mum now. It's Tony."

Lorne accepted the phone from her daughter. "Tony? Is everything okay?"

"Just ringing up to let you know I'm in for a long one tonight."

"Seriously? Why? I hope your client is paying overtime rates?"

Tony chuckled. "Hardly. Hey, we both understand this isn't a nine-to-five sort of job. I've got to go. We're on the move. I'll fill you in when I get back."

"When's that likely to be?" Lorne asked, but Tony's response was the end-call tone ringing in her ear. She placed the phone on the kitchen table and went back to preparing their evening meal. "Maybe he got wind of what we're having for dinner."

Charlie laughed a full belly laugh. "That's hilarious, Mum."

"What is?" Lorne asked, amused and confused by her daughter's reaction.

"Got wind of what we're having. As in the type of wind that goes hand in hand with jacket spuds."

Lorne cringed. "Oh dear, I honestly didn't mean that. Have you got any plans for tonight?" Lately, she'd been concerned by her daughter's reluctance to leave the house at night. Ever since Charlie's best friend had died at a birthday party almost eighteen months ago, she had hardly stepped foot out of the house in the evening. Lorne feared that her daughter might need some form of counselling to get over the incident, but that really wouldn't go down well with Charlie, given her past experience with a counsellor after her abduction by the Unicorn.

"Nope, the usual, listen to music on my iPod. Why?" She nudged her mother's elbow and rested her head on her shoulder. "What did you have in mind? A girlie night in with a soppy movie and chocolate?"

"We can do that if that's really what you want to do, love? Actually, I thought we could go over and see how Carol is doing. What do you think?"

Charlie stood upright again and started chopping a bunch of spring onions. "I don't mind."

Lorne picked up a note of disappointment in her daughter's voice. Rethinking her strategy, she said, "We could see how Onyx has settled into her new home."

Charlie shook her head and groaned. "Nice try, Mum. Onyx has been 'settled into her new home' for over six months now. If you want to go and check up on Carol, I'll tag along, no worries."

"But you'd rather spend some quality time with your mother, given the choice. Is that what you're getting at?"

Charlie's teeth glistened when she turned to grin at Lorne. "It'll be cool to spend time together for a change, like the old days, just you and me."

Lorne thought back to the period of their lives she felt Charlie was referring to and surmised it was before Lorne was involved with Tony, after her divorce from Tom. "You mean when I was between husbands? You don't regret me getting together with Tony, do you, sweetie?"

Charlie turned sharply to face her. "Did I say that? Stop overanalysing my statements. You're hopeless in that respect, Mum. Just accept it the way it was meant. I miss girly time with you. Every young woman feels that at some point in their lives, don't they?"

Lorne leaned over and kissed Charlie's cheek. "Nothing wrong in that at all. I'll finish this off. You go sort out a movie. If you look in the bureau drawer, you might even find a box of chocolates I've stashed away for Christmas."

"Really? You've started shopping early for a change. You usually leave everything to the very last minute."

"I thought I'd be different this year. That doesn't give you the go-ahead to start searching every nook and cranny for your present, either, young lady."

Charlie clutched a hand to her chest. "Would I do that?"

"Yes, you *would*. Although I think you learnt your lesson a few years back after snooping in your grandmother's wardrobe and munching on her Ex-Lax chocolate."

Charlie retched at the thought. "God, don't remind me. I spent two whole days on the loo, if I remember rightly."

Lorne laughed. "That's right. Hey, maybe that particular incident was behind me leaving the Christmas shopping until the last minute over the years."

"Could be. Although, I think I learnt my lesson right then."

"Oh dear, I hope the memory doesn't put you off getting stuck into the chocolates this evening?" Lorne joked with a wink.

"No fear of that. I'll go choose a film. Are you sure you don't need a hand here?"

"Shoo! I'll be fine. I'll just give Carol a ring to see how she is, though, if that's okay?"

"I'll expect dinner in a couple of hours then," Charlie groaned, leaving the kitchen.

Lorne wiped her hands on the tea towel and dialled her friend's number. "Hi, Carol. Just checking in with you."

"Hello, Lorne. You don't need to worry about me. How is the investigation going?"

"Nonsense, I'm concerned about you. Katy and I have been chasing our tails all day. Hopefully, once the *Crimewatch* programme has aired, we'll get a new batch of information that'll lead us to the victim. I don't suppose you've got anything else you'd like to share on that front, have you?"

"I know how bizarre all of this sounds, but this young woman has no intention of leaving me alone, not until her body is found. I did pick up on a couple of initials today that I wanted to run past you. The first is a *C*. Does that fit?"

Lorne nodded as if Carol were standing in the kitchen with her. "It certainly does. Anything else?"

"I'm glad to hear that because this woman was adamant about that. I also picked up on the letter *N*. How's that?"

"Spot on again. Did the spirit just come out and give you the initials, Carol?"

"No. We've been at it all day. She's given me numerous pictures of items and places all with the same initial. You know nothing is ever easy with these guys. Otherwise, I would have won the lottery by now. I'm glad they fit, Lorne. I'll keep working hard with her. She's sure to turn up again later. She's persistent—I'll give her that."

"Not wishing to push my luck, but any chance she can let us know the initials of the man who abducted her? If it was a man. Or who killed her, come to that?"

"I need to take things slowly. You understand, don't you?"

Lorne let out a sigh. "Of course I do. Maybe if I gave you some initials of the suspects on the list we're working our way through. Do you think that would help?"

"I doubt it. You know I don't like working that way. I need to come up with the goods by myself for people like Pete, bless him—and Katy, for that matter—to believe in my abilities. I saw the expression on Katy's face when I was running through my experience with this woman earlier today."

"She doesn't mean anything by it, Carol. You know as well as I do how many sceptics there are in this world. Give Katy time to adjust to how things work, eh?"

"I will. I'll do what I usually do to win people over, Lorne—come up with the facts and the missing pieces for you to slot together. How's Tony's case going? He shouldn't be too long out there tonight."

Lorne laughed. "See, when you come out with things like that, it's pretty difficult to doubt your abilities. Tony rang about twenty minutes ago, told me he was going to be late home. To be honest, we haven't really discussed his case much. I've been too wrapped up in my own work the last few days."

"Okay, one thing I can tell you on his case—it's not what it seems. I don't think it will end in murder or the death of anyone, so you can let Tony know that if you like."

"Brilliant, that will put his mind at rest. Although, after the last few cases he's helped me out on, I'm really not sure he's feeling the 'buzz' of being a PI yet."

Carol sniggered. "I can totally understand that. Tell him to hang in there. I sense some juicier crimes coming his and his partner's way in the near future."

"I'll pass that message on. Well, I better get back to cooking the dinner. Charlie and I are making the most of our freedom tonight."

"Oh no, you're not going to watch *Titanic* again!"

Lorne cupped her hand around the mouthpiece of the phone and whispered, "I damn well hope not. It's a great film. I just wish they hadn't made it so bloody long."

"I hear you on that one. Enjoy your evening, whatever you decide to watch, and look out for the side effects of those jacket spuds, too."

Carol hung up, leaving Lorne staring at the phone.

Charlie appeared in the doorway. "What's wrong?"

"Nothing. That woman never ceases to amaze me. What film have you chosen?"

"*Marley and Me*. Are you up for the tear-jerking finale?"

"Just make sure my wine glass is topped up all the way through. I should be fine then. Let me crack on with this. I'll soon have it finished."

"Hey, I'm not the one holding you up." Charlie spun on her heel and left the kitchen again.

Lorne quickly assembled the ingredients of the meal and lit the oven before pouring both of them a glass of wine. Before long, she and Charlie were tucking into their jacket potatoes and laughing at the exploits of a golden Labrador causing chaos on the screen. By the end of the film, Lorne was feeling maudlin and patted the sofa for Henry to climb up for a cuddle.

The old boy just about managed the task but yelped when he got his leg caught between the cushions.

"Sweetheart, I'm sorry."

Henry licked her face, forgiving her.

Ten minutes later, when the girls were getting ready to go up to bed, an exhausted Tony entered through the back door.

Lorne collapsed into his arms, overwhelmed by the three glasses of red wine she'd consumed. "I missed you tonight, handsome."

Tony wrapped his arms around her and snuggled into her neck. "Well, that's good to know. It would be preferable if you'd actually told me when you were stone-cold sober, but this will have to suffice."

"Cheeky sod. You know I wuve you." She hiccupped and looked up at him, her gaze blurry and an odd sensation sweeping through her tummy. "Twony... I don't feel so good."

Tony swept her up in his arms and took her upstairs to the bathroom. "You stay here. I'll be back after I've checked the kennels and locked up downstairs, all right?"

Her head swam, and she smiled at his swaying figure in the doorway. "Okay, don't be wong."

CHAPTER SEVEN

In the morning, Lorne regretted downing a bottle of wine.

"Oh, God, I feel like crap!" She rolled over, placed her feet on the floor, and held her throbbing head in her open hands.

"And you're expecting sympathy from me?" Tony asked. He crawled behind her and placed his head over her shoulder.

Lorne pulled her head away. "Do you have to shout?"

He jumped off the bed and walked into the bathroom, closing the door behind him.

"Hey, I have to go in there first," she called after him, wincing when the screech in her voice injured her throbbing head further.

"You should've got your arse out of bed quicker then. I'll only be five minutes. A coffee would be most welcome. Thanks, darling," her husband shouted above the noise of the running shower.

Tentatively, Lorne descended the stairs. After greeting Henry with his morning kiss and cuddle, she filled the kettle, slumped into the chair, and waited for the water to boil.

Tony joined her ten minutes later, his hair still damp, and his eyes twinkling with devilment. He waved a finger at her and winked. "That'll teach you not to overindulge on a school night."

Ignoring the jibe, she asked, "Are you starting work early? Is it the same case?"

"Yep, something came to light last night, and Joe and I agreed on a new strategy for today."

"That's a little evasive. What do you mean?"

Tony picked up Lorne's lukewarm coffee, downed it, then crossed the room to the back door. "I'll tell you tonight. I'm hoping it will be an early one today—if things go according to plan, that is. The painkillers are in the bathroom cabinet. You might want to take a packet to work with you. I can't see that wearing off any time soon, Mrs. Warner. Shame on you for getting into such a state."

"Yeah, yeah. It's all Charlie's fault for putting that darn movie on. See you later. Have a good day. Ring me at lunchtime if you can."

"I will. Have a good day. Love you."

Lorne was the last member of the team to arrive at work. Her head still felt as if someone had shoved it in a bubble tied to a set of drums. "What's with all the excitement?"

Katy frowned and approached her. "You look rough. Not feeling too good?"

"Self-inflicted. Hey, you should have laid eyes on me an hour ago."

Katy shook her head, not amused in the slightest. "Taken anything for this self-inflicted punishment, have you?"

"Yep. I'm well on the road to recovery, boss. I promise it won't affect my work."

"It better not, Lorne, for your sake." Katy turned and addressed the rest of the team: "Okay, as we know, the case was shown to the public on *Crimewatch* last night. The important thing is to monitor any calls we receive, giving priority to any sightings of Noelle herself or her car. So far, we have two possible leads that we need to chase up this morning. Let me know right away as the calls happen, okay?"

"What sort of sightings are they?" Lorne asked.

"One said she recognised Noelle. The woman wasn't sure when or where she saw her, though. I'll send Graham out to get a statement from her. The other call was about the car. Again, the information was a little obscure, nothing definitive we can sink our teeth into just yet. Graham, check the locations of the two calls and see if you can fit them in at the same time, will you?"

"Yes, boss." He picked up the two sheets of paper from his desk and studied them. "From what I can tell, they're within a few miles of each other."

"Okay, that's doable this morning, right? Also, can you pinpoint the locations on the map as the calls come in? Let's start forming a picture of possible sightings. It'll help us weed out the ones we shouldn't be wasting our time on—you know, the ones we think might be too far afield."

"The trouble with that is, we can't really discount anything that comes in, boss, not without feeling the wrath of the super, or indeed, Noelle's family. We owe it to them to chase up every lead. Who knows how far the person who abducted Noelle travelled before..." Lorne paused and glanced over her shoulder at the door, just in case any unexpected visitors were lurking there. "Before they dumped her body. If her body was discarded, we still can't rule out the possibility of Noelle being held somewhere. That could turn out to be the remotest part of London for all we know."

"Okay, that's a fair enough point. For now, let's gather the evidence and map everything out. I'd still like you to interview those two callers, Graham," Katy insisted. She pulled Lorne to one side and whispered, "If Carol is to be believed, then I don't want to lead the team down the wrong path."

"I agree. Talking of Carol, I rang her last night, and she came up with two initials."

"Of the attacker?"

"Nope, the victim. She came up with *N* and *C*." Lorne smiled when she noted an impressed eyebrow disappear into her partner's fringe.

"Interesting, Noelle Chesterfield, eh? I don't suppose she could embellish you with the initials of a possible suspect?"

"No such luck. I did ask, though. Maybe something will come through soon. I think she's having a torrid time with the girl's tortured soul." Lorne shrugged. "I don't have a clue how these things work. We'll just need to be patient. I'll ring her when I get home this evening. I told her to take a few days off from work."

"Did you see the programme last night?"

Lorne cringed and admitted she hadn't. "Sorry, Charlie and I made the most of Tony being stuck at work."

"I see, hence the hangover this morning. Well, the show did us proud. The girl who played Noelle was a great likeness, so I envisage a mountain of calls coming our way today. Mind if I talk frankly?"

"Go for it." Lorne feared she knew what her partner was about to say next and prepared herself for a major dressing down.

"I'm not one for going OTT about these kinds of things, but I do draw the line at members of my team showing up for work hungover and looking like they'd spent the night at a zombie's initiation party. If this had arisen with any other team member, I would have sent them home *and* docked their wages."

"I'm sorry, Katy. I've never done it before, and I'll certainly think twice about doing it in the future. I promise it won't affect my work. If it does, you have my permission to dock my wages."

"I'll do more than that, Lorne. I'll have no hesitation in suspending you," she warned. As Katy turned and headed for her office, she shot over her shoulder, "Don't let me down, Sergeant."

"I won't," Lorne called back, regretting it when her words reverberated around the inside of her skull again, punishing her.

Calls dribbled in during the course of the morning. Then, around eleven o'clock, Lorne answered a call that had the potential to break the case wide open. As soon as she hung up, she knocked on Katy's door and entered.

Katy looked up, frowned, and sat back in her chair. "Why did you knock? I'm not mad at you, Lorne. You know you can come in whenever you want to."

"I'd rather knock than have my head chewed off. It's in a delicate state this morning, as you're fully aware. Seriously, I have some amazing news." She smiled and waved the sheet of paper in front of her as she dropped into the spare chair.

"What's that?"

"I think we might have located Noelle's car. In fact, I'm pretty certain we have."

Katy eagerly sat forward. "Really? That's wonderful news. Where?"

"Here's the thing—the car was just about to be crushed. The scrapyard owner watched the programme last night. He recognised the make, colour, and model, and the plate number."

"Wow, that's fortunate. Is it far?"

"About twenty minutes away. I've called forensics. They're on their way over to the site now."

Katy stood and slipped on her jacket. "Come on, let's get over there and see for ourselves. This is brilliant news."

By the time they arrived at the location, forensics had cordoned off the area. Lorne and Katy introduced themselves to the scrapyard owner. He pointed to the vehicle and walked with them to the car.

"Mr. Cheedle, can you tell us a little bit more about the car? Where it was found? How did it come to be here?" Katy asked.

"No problem. I'll have to double check my records to make sure I've got all the facts straight, but from what I can remember, a young guy dropped the car off on the back of a loader. Said it wasn't worth keeping anymore because the engine had died. We get so many cars in here. It was an older model, so I just took his word for it and gave him the scrap value."

Katy glanced at Lorne then back at the short, chubby man. "So you'd have this guy's name and address on record then?"

"Yep, although whether he gave me his real address, I have no way of knowing. I can dig that information out for you."

"That's great. Can you do that for us now?" Lorne asked, eager to see if any of the names on their suspect list matched the man who'd dropped off the vehicle.

The man groaned and retraced his steps back to the porta cabin office near the entrance.

"I bet it turns out to be a fake address and identity. The question is whether the guy found the vehicle after it was abandoned and brought it here just to pick up the scrap money, or was the man who deposited the car here Noelle's abductor?" Lorne said.

Katy nodded. "My thoughts exactly. Another thing that bothers me about this is why the scrapyard didn't log the vehicle at DVLA. He has to, doesn't he?"

"Let's get all the info we need from him first and then pull him up on that," Lorne replied.

The crusher on the other side of the yard whined as it squeezed the life out of an old wreck. Unease gnawed at Lorne's stomach when she was reminded about the case she and Pete had solved involving a gang of men who made it their business to rid the country of all the unwanted racing greyhounds.

"Lorne? Are you okay? You look peaky all of a sudden."

"I'm fine. My mind just revisited an old case. That's all. I'll tell you about it some time."

"I'll hold you to that. Here he comes."

The man reappeared, panting heavily. He handed a piece of paper to Katy. She read the name, shook her head then handed it over to Lorne. She was disappointed that she didn't recognise it, either.

"We'll pay the gentleman a visit. I don't suppose you can give us a description of the man, Mr. Cheedle?"

He rubbed the back of his neck with his right hand. "It was a long time ago."

"Please try. Anything will do. Any distinguishing features, perhaps?" Katy urged.

"Let me think." He closed his eyes for a moment or two then opened them quickly. "A tattoo, here, on his forearm."

"That's great. Of what? Can you remember?"

"No. Some kind of animal maybe. Not one hundred percent certain of that, though."

"That's a start. What about his physique?"

"Well, he was around the six-foot mark, I guess. Skinny-gutted sod, he was."

"Hair colour? Blemished or clear skin? Anything else would really help us form a picture of this man." Katy smiled and distractedly glanced in the direction of Noelle's car, where the two forensics men dressed in white overalls had just opened the driver's door.

"Sorry, that's all you're going to get out of me. I just can't remember that far back. We get loads of people through those gates a week."

"I bet. But how many of them turn up with a car loaded on a trailer?" Katy asked, a tight smile tugging at her lips.

"You'd be surprised," the man replied sharply.

"Okay, I'll have to concede that you can't remember the nitty-gritty facts. How about this then? When a car comes into your yard, aren't you supposed to send the log book to DVLA in Swansea to strike it off the system?"

He frowned and scratched his head. "That's right."

"See, this is our problem. If you had reported the car, struck it off, then maybe our case would have been solved a long time ago. Did the car not ring a bell with you six months ago when the case appeared on the local news?" Katy said.

"For a start, I don't watch the local news or get the local paper, before you ask that one. The only reason the car came to mind last night was because of the show. I did the honest-citizen kind of thing and reported it, and now that you're giving me grief, I'm kinda wishing I hadn't bothered informing you."

"I'm sorry, if that's how it's coming across. We're really appreciative of you contacting us. We're just eager to know the car's whereabouts for the last six months, since the owner was reported missing. If the car was brought here within the first day or two, then it'll narrow our search down. Another question for you, Mr. Cheedle. Do you usually store cars for six months or more? Wouldn't you need to crush them sooner to avoid the yard reaching its full capacity?"

"Ordinarily, yes. But it depends on the make of the car and if it is more valuable to have the car sitting around here or just getting rid. This particular car, we've found useful to have hanging around for the spare-parts value. As for registering it, the guy who brought it in swore blind that he'd sent the paperwork off to DVLA. I didn't have any reason not to believe him about that. He seemed genuine enough to me."

"Then I'll have to accept that. We'll just check on the forensic guys and then get out of your hair. Thanks for your time and for contacting us." Katy dismissed the man, who grudgingly turned and started walking back to his office.

"Let's hope we can find evidence in the car," Lorne said as they strode over to the vehicle.

Katy introduced them both to the forensics team. "I know you've only just started, but have you found anything yet?"

The taller of the two men, who'd introduced himself as Jim, smiled and tapped his nose with his index finger. "As it happens, yes. From what we were told about the victim's height, it would appear that the seat position has been altered."

Lorne snorted. "That figures, if the bloke who dropped it off here got in the vehicle. Any way of knowing how tall the person was? A rough guess perhaps?"

"I'd say between five ten and six two, and that would be a very rough guess off the top of my head. The next step is to look for any possible DNA, although given the location, I'm sure that will prove to be plentiful and not the kind of DNA we're after…"

"Hold on a moment. What do we have here?" The other forensic guy pulled something out from under the driver's seat and held it up for all to see.

Lorne gasped. "A handbag. Noelle's handbag?"

"Looks that way. I'll get a pair of gloves for you both so you can peep inside before we take it back to the lab."

Katy nudged Lorne. "This could be just what we need to draw this to a conclusion."

"I agree. Good job we came down here. It would have been days before we got to hear about this evidence otherwise."

Katy glanced at her watch. "We'll gather what we can then shoot off. I want to return to Dilbert's house, see if we can find him home during the day."

"Good idea."

Jim held out two sets of plastic gloves for Lorne and Katy, then he laid out a large clear evidence bag on the floor and emptied the contents of the handbag on top of it.

A small address book caught Lorne's attention immediately. "Mind if I take a look?"

Jim handed the hardback book to her, and she leafed through its many entries.

"Looks like she was a popular girl. It's a shame we couldn't get to work on this immediately." She smiled at Jim in hope, more than expectation, and was greeted with a stern shake of his head.

"Nope, not going to happen for a few more days yet, ladies. No amount of begging will alter that decision, either."

Katy shrugged. "You can't blame a girl for trying, Jim. What else is in there?"

"A purse." He opened the zipped compartment of the red purse and ran his gloved hand down the credit and debit cards in the slotted fabric area. "Looks like a fair few cards here. Do we know what the young lady did for a living?"

"Primarily, she was a student, but to make ends meet, she performed at a pole-dancing club a few nights a week."

"It's such a shame when students have to step out of their comfort zones and lower themselves to be involved in such careers. I can't ever see universities explaining the complexities of studying with them full-time, 'Come study with us, exorbitant fees of over thirty grand, but hey, you can always go and show off your body parts to pay for our fees.'"

"You're right there. The problem is, the girl's parents had no idea she had this job. The shock must have been horrendous for them when they learned what she was having to endure just to survive being a student," Lorne stated, glad that Charlie had never wanted to get involved with higher education and was doing so well running her own business caring for the dogs on a daily basis. Handing over the day-to-day running to Charlie had given her a purpose in life that many teenagers had to wait until they were in their thirties to obtain.

"It's a worrying fact that they have to do things so degrading just to get an education. Oh, look, don't get me started. My girl is eighteen. I have this dilemma coming up next year when she goes off to uni. The thing is, I'd rather get a second job than have her degrade herself in such a way."

"Then you're one in a million, Jim. Like I said, Noelle's parents were totally unaware of what was going on in their daughter's life, until it was too late. What else is in the purse?" Lorne asked, peering over his shoulder.

"Looks like she had a fair amount of cash on her. Would that be tips from the club where she worked?" Jim suggested.

Katy nodded. "Might be. Okay, if we're looking at three suspects from the CCTV footage at the club the night before she disappeared, this proves that they were after Noelle from the very beginning."

"Because of the money left in her purse, you mean?" Lorne said.

"It has to be. If her attack had been a genuine attempt to rob her, then why was her jewellery still at her flat and the money left untouched in her purse? Okay, we have to be somewhere else soon, Jim. Is there anything else of significance inside the handbag?"

He tipped out the remainder of the contents and shook his head. "There doesn't appear to be. A lipstick, compact mirror, a few pens, and a notepad. Nothing else."

"Okay, we're going to leave you to it then. Can you promise me that you'll treat the address book as urgent and pass it over to us ASAP?"

"Of course, you have my word on that. If we find anything else, I'll be sure to ring and let you know." Jim tucked the items back in the handbag and placed it in another evidence bag, along with the evidence bag he'd tipped out the contents of the handbag onto.

"Thanks, guys. Speak soon. *Very* soon," Katy said, emphasising how urgent the matter was before they left the yard and got back in the car.

Once they arrived at Dilbert's residence, Lorne could tell instantly someone was at home or had at least visited. The curtains that had been open before were drawn. "Looks like we're in luck," Lorne noted, stepping out of the vehicle.

"All right. Let's be cautious about this, bearing in mind what went on with Simms."

"You don't need to remind me," Lorne said, miffed that Katy kept bringing up the subject that she'd made the unforgiveable mistake of letting a suspect slip through her fingers, not once, but twice.

"Calm down. I wasn't having a dig. I'll forgive you snapping at me given your fragile state this morning."

"Thanks. I appreciate that," Lorne replied grudgingly.

Katy knocked on the door.

Lorne watched the window carefully, looking for any sign of curtain twitching by the occupant. "There, he's seen us."

Katy rapped on the door a second time then bent down and shouted through the letterbox. "Mr. Dilbert, it's the police. We'd like a chat with you, if that's okay? Shit! Looks like he's going out the back way."

They spun around and frantically looked left and right for a possible alleyway. "Here!" Lorne pointed at a gap in between the houses on her left.

Katy and Lorne bolted down the narrow passageway to the rear of the properties.

"Shit! He just rounded the corner. I'm going to call for backup." Katy slowed her pace, dug out her phone, and dialled the station.

"I'll carry on," Lorne shouted, squeezing past her colleague and upping her speed. The pounding on the concrete surface did little to ease the pain in her head. She had to dig deep into her resolve to combat the urge to throw up. Keeping a constant eye both up ahead and at the wheelie bins she passed in case the suspect had hidden behind one of them, she continued through the maze-like area until she reached the end and was confronted by a patch of open grassland, a community playing field of some sort.

Lorne glanced over her shoulder while she caught her breath just as Katy halted beside her.

"They're sending out a couple of cars. Did you see which way he went?"

Lorne shook her head and gulped in a lungful of fresh air. "No. Shall we make a start? Looks like some kind of changing room over there."

"Good place as any to start."

They marched over to the newly decorated wooden structure on the edge of the field near the car park. Lorne armed herself with her pepper spray and gingerly approached the front door. She tried the handle and found the door locked. Something caught her attention in the car park just beyond. Lorne nudged Katy. "Did you hear that? It came from behind the recycle bins."

"Yep, let's take a look."

Dilbert emerged from behind the bins before they could get within ten feet of his position. He laughed, gave them the bird, and bolted again.

"Damn! Where the bloody hell is that backup?"

Lorne and Katy chased the suspect as he ran through the parked cars and hopped over a fence. Then someone yelled out in pain. "Quick, the idiot has hurt himself."

In the distance, sirens approached. Lorne pointed to the end of the fence, and they tore around the panel. Lorne spotted the suspect lying on the ground, tears streaming down his face.

"Help me. Don't just stand there. Call me an ambulance, you idiots."

Katy punched 999 into her phone.

You're an ambulance, Lorne wanted to say, but she bit down on that witty retort and said instead, "They're on their way. It's not always a good idea to run from the police, is it?" she said smugly.

He spat on the ground close to Lorne's feet. "Well, I didn't know there was going to be a bloody boulder sitting on the other side of the fence, did I?"

"Lucky break for us then." Lorne laughed. "No pun intended."

The youngster spat again and fixed her with an evil glare.

"While we have your undivided attention, do you mind telling us why you took off like that?"

"'Cause you guys are forever knocking on my door, causing me aggro."

"We are? Have you ever asked yourself why that is, Mr. Dilbert? We don't tend to 'cause ag' to innocent people."

He snorted and narrowed his eyes. "You expect me to believe *that*. I've made a few mistakes in my life and get pounced on by your lot all the frigging time, whether I'm guilty or not. What's bloody fair about that?"

Lorne hitched up a shoulder as Katy rejoined them. "Shit happens, I guess. If you see fit to run every time a copper knocks at your door, what are we supposed to glean from that?"

"Well, I ain't guilty. Where's that effing ambulance? Just 'cause you've got me here, it doesn't mean I'm gonna answer your questions."

"That's up to you. It'll only make matters worse for you if you don't. Your choice—I'd advise you to make the right one." Katy gave him a dazzling smile and a nonchalant shrug.

Two Panda cars pulled into the car park and four uniformed officers joined them.

"Well, as you can see, gentlemen, we managed to apprehend the suspect all by ourselves. We're waiting for the ambulance to arrive now. You can head back to the station. Thanks, all the same."

Disgruntled, the PCs hopped back in their vehicles and departed the scene just as the paramedics screeched to a halt in the car park.

One paramedic trotted up to them with his medical bag at his side while the other, a female, opened up the rear door of the ambulance and pulled out a stretcher.

"Hello, ladies. What do we have here then?" the older male paramedic asked. He bent down beside the suspect to check out the man's injury for himself.

"The foolish young man vaulted the fence in his haste to get away from us and came a cropper. I suspect he's broken his ankle," Katy said.

The paramedic nodded. "Looks like a break to me. A hospital trip is in order here."

Dilbert slapped the ground. "Aww... damn. Can't you just bandage it up or somethin'? I got places to go and people to see. Ain't got time to be laid up in a hospital bed."

"Tough. The last thing we want is you suing us for negligence." Katy told him. She winced when the paramedics cut Dilbert's jeans open to reveal the bone jutting out of his skin just above the ankle.

"Man, look at that. Jesus, that's well and truly busted. Hey, lady, I might not be able to sue you for negligence, but I'll make sure I pin something on you. I'm innocent, and you still gave chase. *You* effing did this to me, and I'm gonna make sure you bloody pay for what you've done."

Katy glanced at Lorne and then the paramedic, who was suppressing a grin.

"Since when did innocent people run away from the police?" he said.

"Precisely," Lorne agreed. "I'd advise you to keep your threats to yourself, Mr. Dilbert, because they're not going to wash with us."

After struggling to erect the temperamental stretcher that appeared to get stuck halfway a few times before finally playing ball, the female paramedic joined them.

"Okay, let's see if we can strap this up just to make it more comfortable for the journey and to keep the wound clean," the paramedic attending the suspect said.

Katy and Lorne stepped away from the scene for a conflab. "What do you suggest we do now?" Katy asked.

"We're going to have to accompany him to the hospital. Whether we'll get the chance to interview him there is hard to say. He'll probably be taken down to theatre as soon as he arrives. Time is getting on. It could turn out to be an all-nighter, and for what? If he's saying he's innocent, we could end up wasting valuable time just by babysitting him at the hospital."

"You're right. Hey, he might be innocent, but we haven't laid any claims at his door yet. Knowing he has a past record for sexual assault, we can hardly deem him as totally innocent, can we?"

"Good point." Lorne slapped her fist against her thigh. "We're wasting time, though. Can't we assign a uniformed officer to watch over him at the hospital and pick up the slack in the morning?"

Katy ran a finger across her lips as she thought. "It would make sense. Let me ring the station, see what I can arrange at short notice."

Lorne went back to watch over the suspect, who was going for the award in the world's worst patient category, crying out and even threatening to thump the paramedic caring for him at one point.

"Calm down. Let the man do his job. The quicker the wound is dressed, the faster we can all get out of here."

"But he's hurting me," Dilbert whined like a ten-year-old boy.

"Can you give him a painkiller of sorts?" she asked the paramedic.

"Already done it. It'll kick in soon. Providing the patient is patient that is."

Everyone laughed, except the suspect.

"Crap. What am I? Someone for you to take a pop at, to test your frigging jokes on to pass the time away? Get a life," he retorted aggressively.

"That's sorted," Katy said, coming back to the group. "I've arranged for a uniformed officer to take care of Mr. Dilbert at the hospital. We have to get back to the station. We'll drop by and see you in the morning to interview you. Don't even think about trying to leave the hospital before we've had a chance to chat. Got that?"

The man tutted and slapped the ground again. "Like I've got a bloody choice."

"We'll accompany you to the hospital grounds and then head off. All right?" Katy told the paramedics, who looked relieved to hear the news.

Dilbert continued to cry out in pain for the next ten minutes. He issued threats and shouted expletives as the paramedics tried their best to make their patient more comfortable. Eventually, his cries died down to a whimper once the painkillers kicked in. After the paramedics loaded Dilbert in the back of the ambulance, Katy and

Lorne followed them to the hospital in their vehicle. Once the suspect was safely delivered, they drove back to the station.

After bringing the team up to date with what had taken place during the afternoon, Katy gave everyone permission to head home for the day.

Lorne called home before she left the station.

Charlie answered the phone, sounding relaxed. "Hi, love. It's me. Just setting off home now. Do you need me to stop off for anything?"

"Mmm… fish and chips would be good. Just kidding." Charlie laughed. "Tony's still out. He rang earlier, said he'd be home about six thirty."

"That's great. I should be with you about that time, too. Have you heard from Carol today?"

"No. I meant to call her at lunchtime, but something happened to distract me."

"Nothing major, I hope?"

"No. One of the dogs was sick. He's all right now, though. No need for you to worry. I gave him one of those special pills we got from the vet."

"Well done, you. All right, look, the chippie is quite close to Carol's house. I'll drop in and see her first. Are you okay with that? I shouldn't be any later than quarter to seven. Will your hunger pangs last that long?"

"Yeah, I'll grab a biscuit to stave off the pain until then. Give my love to Carol and tell her I've enjoyed her not being here today. I've had no one to boss around." Charlie chuckled.

"I'll pass that on. See you later." Lorne hung up and tapped her forehead with her fingertips.

"What's wrong?" Katy asked, just stepping out of her office.

"Damn, we forgot to ring the Chesterfields to tell them about Noelle's car."

Katy waved her hand. "Go. I can do that before I head off. Enjoy your evening."

Grateful that Katy took onus of the situation, she said farewell to the team and set off.

CHAPTER EIGHT

Lorne hadn't rung Carol to inform her of her imminent arrival, and by the looks of things, she thought she might regret that decision. Carol's house was in darkness, except for the soft glow of candlelight emanating from the lounge window. Lorne shuddered at the spooky scene she saw inside, of Carol sitting at the table in a trance-like state, and knocked on the door. It took another round of knocking to jolt Carol out of her trance and to open the front door.

Carol thrust the door open, grabbed Lorne's forearm, and yanked her into the house. "Quick, take a seat. I'm in conversation with Noelle. I just hope your appearance hasn't put her off."

Lorne cringed. Being part of a séance hadn't figured highly on her evening agenda, but Carol was virtually forcing her to take part. She leaned in and whispered, "So, she's finally divulged her name then?"

"Yes, the information is coming through slowly, as I suggested it would. Spirits have to learn they can trust us before they reveal intimate details about their past lives. Now sit there and be quiet. I'll see if I can call her forward again."

"Do you have to? Can't you tell me what she said and then pick up where you left off after I've gone? I only dropped by to see how you are. Charlie and Tony will be expecting their tea, Carol."

"Nonsense, the chip shop is only up the road, Lorne. Now, hush. Spirits surrounding us, please step forward."

Lorne's eyes roamed the semi-darkened room while her stomach tied itself into knots. Straining her eyesight, she discovered a dull light starting to come towards them from its hideaway in the corner of the room. As the orb drew closer, its glow grew more intense and vivid. Lorne reached for Carol's hand, needing support. Carol wrapped her hands around Lorne's.

"Noelle, that's it, child. Come closer. Lorne won't hurt you. If anything, she is trying her hardest to help you. Come closer, dear."

Lorne held her breath as the light came to a halt approximately two feet from where she sat. Carol squeezed harder, obviously trying to reassure her. It didn't work—Lorne's heart rate escalated so fast that she thought she was going to pass out. She struggled to breathe properly.

"Breathe deeply. In through your nose and out through your mouth. She won't harm you. All Noelle wants to do is guide you," Carol said out of the corner of her mouth.

Lorne gulped and nodded, then carried out Carol's instructions.

"Noelle has just arrived this evening, Lorne. She's trying to tell me where her body lies. She's very distressed about her death, as you can imagine. I've told her how important it is for her to help us locate her body. If we can find it, her move towards the light will be instantaneous. At the moment, her restless soul is unwilling to move on."

At a loss for what to say in the company of the spirit, Lorne finally swallowed hard and whispered, "I see."

She understood some parts of Carol's work, but not the interaction with a spirit. Usually, when Carol contacted a spirit, she closed her eyes and rocked back and forth. However, Carol seemed far more relaxed than normal, conversing with the spirit as if Noelle were a long-lost friend. Lorne remained mesmerised by the dull light, which, thankfully, hadn't manifested into anything scarier than that, yet.

"Come, Noelle, be strong. Lorne will listen with an open mind to what you have to say."

Lorne turned to look at Carol, thinking for a moment that her friend had finally lost her mind. Then a faint voice spoke close to her ear, almost making her lose the contents of her bowels. With a pounding heart, she slowly twisted her head to look at the spirit— and was shocked to see the faint outline of the girl's face barely inches from her own. Carol clenched Lorne's hand, no doubt sensing that she wanted to bolt from the room.

"A hill," the haunting voice said.

"Where, Noelle? Where is this hill?" Carol asked.

Lorne gathered her wits, stuck a hand in her pocket, and withdrew her notebook and pen.

The spirit's voice dulled, and a whimper filled the room. "I don't know," she said over and over again.

"All right. Forget that for now," Carol said, smiling.

Lorne sensed that her friend intended to put the spirit at ease once more. In spite of what was taking place, Lorne felt her own fears subside a little. She even discovered she had enough courage to ask the spirit a question of her own. "Can you give us anything else about the area, Noelle? Do you recognise it? Have you ever visited the area prior… to your death?" she added, hating to put the facts so bluntly.

"No. Never visited," the subdued voice responded.

Carol seemed happy for Lorne to continue asking the questions and remained quiet, listening to them interact.

"Who did this, Noelle? Can you tell us anything about him? I take it the culprit was a male?"

"Yes and no."

Confused, Lorne glanced at Carol, who was urging her on with widened eyes.

"I don't understand. Can you be more specific?"

After several silent moments, Lorne thought the spirit might have disappeared, but then she saw the girl had shifted and seemed to be pacing from one corner to another.

"Yes, male. No, I thought I knew him, but…"

Lorne's confusion swelled as the spirit's words drifted off. *Do I push for answers? Clearer answers? Or do I sit back and let her talk on her terms, at her own pace?* Having never contacted anyone from the other side before, she found the situation difficult. She only hoped that Carol would know if things were going badly and come to her aid if that happened.

The spirit let out a long, shuddering breath. "It's all confused. I'm riddled with confusion."

That makes two of us, sweetheart. "I know, but the more you tell us, the quicker you can continue on your journey. Please try, Noelle."

Carol winked and gave a brief nod, reassuring Lorne.

"All I can tell you is what I see."

"That's great. Reveal what you can, Noelle. I'm used to piecing clues together to build a case. Take all the time you need."

The young woman drifted towards them again and stood alongside Lorne, close to the table. "I see a hill, gravestones, a bridge of sorts, a beautiful tree—the kind I've admired for years. The name of the tree escapes me."

Lorne scribbled down the details in her notebook as Noelle delivered the clues, sometimes fast and frenetic, and at other times, slow and methodical. Nevertheless, Lorne felt relieved that she was getting what she perceived were valuable clues and insights into the case. She guessed she would find out over the coming days just how accurate those clues turned out to be. At least she was beginning to feel more comfortable in the company of the spirit. That in itself helped considerably. She was beginning to learn when to pull back and give the spirit time to recover between questions as the conversation continued.

She proceeded with caution. "That's brilliant, Noelle. You have provided us with some superb clues. Now, can you dig even deeper? Try and tell me the name of the person…"

"Who murdered me?"

Lorne sighed heavily. "Yes, name the person who took your life."

"No. That's the one thing I'm finding impossible to conjure up." Noelle's spirit walked away from the table again and back to the corner of the room, where she began to pace.

"I'm sorry. I didn't mean to push you," Lorne said quietly.

"I can't tell you that." the spirit replied, her voice strained with emotion.

"Then relax. Don't search for the name now. Maybe it will come to you in the future. Please don't worry. You've given me enough to be going on with for the moment." Lorne turned to Carol, her mouth twisting, at a loss what to say next.

Carol took over. "Noelle, I've seen this many times before. Please do not blame yourself. You're too close. Sometimes, life seems way too complicated. You need to stop trying so hard. The answer will come eventually."

Lorne clicked her fingers. "I know! What if I throw some names at you, people we believe might be connected with the case? Will that help?"

"You can try." Again Noelle floated back to her position by Lorne's side, as if eager to help.

"Okay, let's give this a shot." She flipped back through her notebook to refresh her mind. Then she had another idea—she would add a few names of her male colleagues to the mix as a kind of test to see how the spirit reacted. "All right the first name is Colin Simms. Does that name have any significance?"

Silence circulated the room as the spirit thought. Finally, Noelle answered, "No, I'm sorry. Try another."

Lorne looked down at her notebook, but the name she intended to try next wasn't written on the pages of her book because it belonged to one of her team. "Graham Barlow."

Again, the name was greeted with silence before Noelle let out a long breath and said, "No. Why can't I remember?"

Lorne mentally kicked herself for trying to trick the spirit. "Don't punish yourself, Noelle. What about Gary James?"

Again, the spirit thought in silence. "I recognise the name. Where do I know the name from?" she asked then answered herself, "From the club, right?"

"That's correct. He lives with his mother. Does that help you place him?" Lorne offered.

"Yes, I remember. He's a sweet guy. He jumped on the stage to shake my hand once or twice. He wasn't connected to what happened to me."

Lorne again tried to pass off one of her colleague's names, and like before, the spirit denied recognising the person, which came as a relief to Lorne. "Okay, let's try this one—Chris Dilbert."

She walked back and forth a few steps. "The name is familiar to me. Can we keep him on standby? I'm not getting the urge to say that he's definitely the one."

"Of course, but I have no other suspects."

"That's a shame," Noelle said. "I don't feel any of those names are any good. Why can't I be more certain about things?"

Carol cleared her throat to speak, and Lorne nodded. "Give it time. It's too raw. You're keen to lock out anything to do with this person. It's natural—he has stripped you of your life. Be patient, and it will come."

Obviously exhausted after sharing the information with them, Noelle's spirit vanished. Lorne and Carol both expelled long breaths and relaxed into their chairs.

"Well, I hadn't anticipated walking into something like that when I chose to pay you a visit."

Carol laughed, easing the tension in her taut features. "We'd only just commenced our session five minutes before you arrived. The poor child had been sobbing her heart out. She's still very traumatised by what took place. It will be difficult for her to transfer to the other side until her murder is resolved."

"We're doing our best, Carol, but with little evidence to hand we're not getting very far. Although, damn, maybe I should have told Noelle this—we located her car today. We're sure that discovery will help solve this case much quicker."

"Yes, you should have mentioned it, Lorne."

"I know. How dumb am I? Don't answer that. Shit, here's another dumb thing for you to consider. I even had a rough identity, at least a few characteristics of the man who dumped her car."

"Oh, Lorne, that would have prompted her memory so much."

"I'm sorry. In my defence, that was my first real encounter with a spirit. My brain kind of went into meltdown when I saw her in the room."

"That's understandable. Hey, now you've had this experience, you'll be more open to the spirits around you, like Pete and your father."

Lorne's eyes welled up with tears. "Really? Are you saying that I'll be able to communicate openly with them in the future?"

"It's not beyond the realms of possibilities, love. Pete has even helped you out on a few cases since his death, hasn't he?"

"Yes, he has. You're right. One question for you in that case?"

Carol chortled. "Here goes. Go on."

Lorne's brow furrowed. "Just thinking about what is going on with Noelle and her inability to cross over—why haven't Dad and Pete done that yet?"

"That's the confusing part. Some tortured souls remain in the atmosphere to avenge their deaths. They feel trapped, unable to move on. Then there are the spirits who have a great affinity to someone still living and they find it impossible to leave that person."

"Are you saying that these spirits stick around to act like someone's guardian angel? To protect their loved ones?"

Carol nodded and placed her hand on top of Lorne's. "Pete loved you, Lorne. You thought he loved you like a sister, but you couldn't be more wrong. It was so much more than that."

A tear trickled down her cheek, and she covered her mouth with her hand to suppress the sob on the edge of escaping.

"Say something. Surely you had an inkling about the depths of his feelings for you?"

Lorne shook her head, momentarily dumbstruck. "I had no idea. I gave that man hell at times. Yes, I loved him, too, but not in the same way I loved Tom or Tony. I always regarded him as my brother, not a possible lover. My God, I hope this doesn't sour the memory I have of him."

"You're being ridiculous! Why should it sour the relationship you once had?"

"Look, Carol, this all might be the most natural thing in the world for you, but I'm still getting used to your 'wacky' world. I know you're not going to take offence at me calling it that because I've heard you hint at your world being in the same light on many occasions."

"You're right. I have. We're both tired, and you have a hungry family to get home to. Let's call it a day now."

Lorne hugged her friend and planted a kiss on her cool cheek. "Why don't you come back with me? Spend the night. Hopefully, the spirits will leave you alone to catch up on some sleep if you're away from here."

"That's kind. I think I should be here, though, just in case Noelle feels the urge to reach out with more information. That's important right now, yes?"

"All right, I'm not happy about your decision, but I know when I'm beaten. Take care and ring me, day or night, if you need to chat about anything. Okay?"

Carol nodded and escorted Lorne to the front door. "I'll ring you tomorrow if I have any news."

The second Lorne stepped out into the fresh night air, she felt as if a weight had been lifted from her shoulders. She waved to Carol and drove to the fish-and-chip shop, recapping the weird events she'd just encountered at her friend's house. She made a mental note to get out a local map when she got home and look up some of the details Noelle had given her. She knew Tony wouldn't be happy about her working at home, but he would understand once she told him what had occurred at Carol's house.

With her tummy rumbling due to the smell of battered cod and chips filling the car, she arrived at the house at the same time Tony pulled up into the drive.

He greeted her with a pensive look and a peck on the cheek. "Good day?"

"So-so. What about you? I'm guessing it wasn't too hot being trapped in a car all day, spying through a set of binoculars," she teased as they walked into the kitchen.

Charlie grabbed the wrapped food and tore open the paper. "I'm starving with a capital *S*. Have you smothered them in vinegar?"

"Yes, Charlie, I have. Did you warm up the plates?" Lorne asked, raising a questioning eyebrow.

"Oops, I forgot. I'm okay, I'll eat mine out of the paper. Can I go upstairs?"

"If you must. I need to have a chat with Tony anyway."

Charlie's eyes narrowed. "Sounds intriguing. Maybe I'll stick around and eavesdrop for a while."

"And maybe you won't. Go!" Lorne turned Charlie by the shoulders and gently shoved her towards the hallway.

"Charlie's right. Consider my interest piqued."

"Let's eat first before my stomach really starts objecting. I'm warning you now that I might need to work after dinner. I'm sure you'll understand why when I tell you what took place tonight."

"Hey, no problem. Can I help at all? I need to keep my brain active before it seizes up. Maybe I'm just not cut out to be a snooping PI."

"Nonsense, you're bound to have these kinds of cases crop up now and again. Come on, let's eat."

They took their fish and chips, still in the paper, and settled onto the couch. In between mouthfuls, Lorne relayed her experience.

"Seriously? Not sure I would have been as understanding as you in similar circumstances." He shuddered. "So, what do you intend doing after we've eaten then?"

"Well, Noelle mentioned a few things relating to where she's buried. That's what Carol and I are presuming anyway. I want to study a map of the area where her car was found to see if I can recognise a possible burial site."

"I see. That makes sense," Tony replied with a light smile.

"Do you want to tell me what went on with your day?"

"It was crap. This woman is no more having an affair than I am."

"How strange. Surely you've got to tell your client that, haven't you?"

Tony stifled a yawn. "See? Just thinking about my case bores me rigid. Joe and I have both told our client that he's totally wrong about his wife. He just won't listen. I'm not sure how long we can keep taking the fool's money. I don't think we're ever going to satisfy him."

"You're going to have to get your point across more succinctly then. Have you given him photographic evidence?"

"Of what? Her coming and going into her place of work? Because that's all it boils down to, really. Yes, she's left the office briefly. Of course she has. However, in all the time we've been following her, we've never seen her meet up with another man."

"Then you're going to have to speak up and tell him you're moving on to another case."

"I know you're right. I'll chat to Joe tomorrow, see if he has any ideas how to get out of this mess." Tony relieved Lorne of her chip paper and took the rubbish into the kitchen. He returned moments later with a can of beer for himself and a glass of wine for Lorne.

"Yikes, not sure I should succumb after last night's debacle."

He thrust the glass into her hand. "One glass isn't going to kill you. Shall I dig out the map?"

"Would you?" She pointed at the drawer in the sideboard. "I think it's in there."

Tony found the dog-eared map while Lorne retrieved her notebook from her handbag.

"So, what are we looking for?" Tony asked.

"Let's see." She ran her hand down the page and tapped her finger. "It's a little sketchy… all right, let's see about this. A hill was the first clue."

"Okay, well that particular clue by itself isn't that helpful, considering the landscape of the area. What else have you got?"

"Hmm… gravestones."

"Interesting. Do you think the spirit was referring to her place of rest? Maybe upon reflection, I could have rephrased that better."

"I don't think so. She wouldn't have a gravestone of her own, would she?"

"True enough."

They searched every inch of the map and discovered thirty or so large graveyards in the London area alone.

"Well, I think we can push that particular clue aside for now. Okay, what about this? A bridge of sorts and a beautiful tree that she couldn't put a name to."

"That's helpful—not. Let's try and piece all the clues together and see what we can find." Tony downed half his can of beer and leaned forward for a closer look at the ordinance survey map.

After another half an hour of intense searching, Lorne threw herself back on the sofa. "It's hopeless. God, if only the spirit would give us the culprit's name. Now that piece of information would get this case wrapped up in an instant."

"Is there any reason why she's unable to do that? Hark at me, getting all frustrated with a spook. The other variety, I mean." Tony laughed, referring to the nickname the general public call MI5 and MI6 operatives.

"I asked the same question. Apparently, it's not uncommon for victims, or the spirits of the victims, to block out their aggressor's name. They don't want to consider themselves as dead, refuse to believe it in most cases," Lorne told him sadly.

"I never thought I'd ever hear myself saying that I have empathy with a spirit, but I do." Tony shook his head then took another sip of beer.

"I know. I feel the same way. I did go through the names of the people we're regarding as suspects with Noelle, without much success. I thought hearing the names might jolt something in her memory, if spirits have memories. God, I'm so confused dealing with this side of things. I'm more than happy to step back and let Carol take control."

"Okay, concentrate. We can mark any areas with two or more of the features you say Noelle supplied you with, and perhaps you and your team can visit the sites tomorrow," Tony suggested.

"Agreed." Jotting down the areas in her notebook, Lorne was pleased by their evening's achievements by the time bedtime came a-calling.

CHAPTER NINE

Feeling brighter than she had on the previous day at first light, Lorne walked into the station, whistling the melody of a hit song in the chart.

"Now that's more like the Lorne Warner we know and love," Katy observed when she joined the rest of the team in the incident room.

"I have a reason to be cheerful, sort of."

"That sounds ominous. Let's have it?"

Lorne marched over to the whiteboard and began writing down the significant details she'd stumbled across at Carol's, along with Noelle's possible whereabouts within their patch. The whole team looked on with a mixture of interest and guarded scepticism when Lorne revealed how she had come up with the information. She held her hands up as she spoke. "I know, I know… it sounds bizarre. Hey, believe me when I say it was one of the weirdest times I've ever been forced to experience. Don't judge just yet, eh? Let's at least look into the clues Noelle has furnished us with before we discount them out of hand, yes?"

Katy joined Lorne at the board. "You're deadly serious about this. Aren't you?"

"Absolutely. I trust Carol implicitly, and after seeing this spirit with my own eyes, I would be foolish to ignore what she has to offer. Let's face it—what else do we have right now?"

"Well, this morning, first thing, I want us to go back to the hospital to question Dilbert. Other than that, not a lot. I'm still not sold on following this route to solve this case, though, Lorne. What about our reputation? We're under the spotlight enough with this cold case as it is. Following this crazy idea and using the leadership of the deceased victim to bring the case to a conclusion is only going to make our superiors question our judgements, in more ways than one."

"I know it's not ideal, but with nothing else really to grab our attention, we'd be idiots not to pounce on this. We can always say that we refused to give up on any leads. Just give it the morning. What have we got to lose?" Lorne pleaded, her gaze scanning the rest of her colleagues.

Katy turned to the team and shrugged. "What do you think, guys? Is it worth our time going along these lines, or not?"

AJ shrugged. "I'm open to investigating the possibilities. Like Lorne said, there's little else on the table for us to sink our teeth into at present."

Katy rubbed her chin between her thumb and forefinger as she pondered. "Just the morning, right?"

Lorne smiled. "Just the morning. If you're agreeable, the team could split up and investigate each of the locations."

"Let me think things over while I plough through the post. In the meantime, Lorne, can you make up a possible itinerary for us to tackle ourselves once we've finished with Dilbert this morning? That way, the team can remain here and keep working through the backgrounds of the suspects, *et cetera*, and deal with any extra calls coming in from the TV programme. AJ, I'd like you to keep trawling through the CCTV discs, and, Karen, I want you to keep pestering forensics for the results of Noelle's car."

The team agreed, then Katy disappeared into her office. Almost an hour later, she emerged. "How are things going?" she asked Lorne.

"In one word—slowly. We've chased up everything you asked us to and come up with major negatives on all fronts."

"Okay, we should head over to the hospital; see what Dilbert has to say for himself, yes?" Katy said, wafting through the incident room, expecting Lorne to follow her out to the car.

In the hallway, Katy almost ran into Chief Roberts, who was walking towards them. "In a rush, are you, Inspector?"

"Always. Were you on the way to see me?" Katy asked him as Lorne joined them.

"Not really. I wanted a quick word with Lorne, actually, but if there's somewhere you have to be, then it can wait."

Katy and Lorne shared a hesitant glance. Lorne was eager to hear what Sean wanted to share with her. However, she knew how tight their schedule was.

Sean raised his hand. "No need to feel awkward, ladies. My news will keep. Go catch yourselves some criminals."

"Thanks. We've got a lot to do today. We're on our way to the hospital to interview a potential suspect who tried absconding yesterday." Katy offered him an awkward smile.

"And how did he manage to be admitted to hospital? Which one of you is to blame for that?" Sean asked, giving each of them a wink.

"No one. It was an unfortunate accident. I was trailing him, and he decided to jump a fence. Ended up busting his ankle. We're hoping they've operated on him by now," Lorne explained, her cheeks heating up as she spoke.

"And you say he's a suspect in the Chesterfield case?"

"Yep. One of three or four we're looking into at the moment. I've promised her parents that we'll wrap the case up by the end of the week," Katy informed the chief.

"You're that confident?"

"Yes and no."

"Meaning what exactly?" Sean leaned against the wall and folded his arms.

Katy glanced at Lorne again and raised an eyebrow as if asking for her permission to tell him about Carol's intervention.

"I'll let Lorne fill you in."

Lorne's eyes widened, and she blustered, "Gee, thanks. All right. I know you're going to find this incredibly hard to believe, but Carol, my psychic friend, is being an indispensable help to us. When I paid her a visit last night, I was greeted by Noelle Chesterfield's spirit."

He launched himself off the wall and began pacing the width of the narrow hallway. "Is that what it has come down to? Your detective skills relying heavily on a spirit?"

"I said you'd find it incredulous. I did at first, I can assure you. To be honest, I was scared shitless when the spirit first appeared. We're going to be up against it today, time-wise. After we finish at the hospital, we'll turn our hand to searching this afternoon, following the clues she's given us. She's determined to help us discover her body. To be fair, we've accomplished far more in the last few days than Travers and Campbell did in a few months. Katy and I decided not to divulge 'our secret source,' knowing the kind of backlash you and possibly the super would give us. If Carol and Noelle fulfil their ambition by leading us to Noelle's body, perhaps you and the super will start regarding psychics and their abilities to help advise the police more in future cases."

"I know you've dealt with this woman over the years and benefited from her abilities. However, I have to reiterate the need to be able to back up anything she says with evidence of the concrete and irrefutable variety. Is that in your remit?" Sean frowned, his gaze shifting between Lorne and Katy.

Katy answered first. "Let's just say that we're doing our best. I'd also like to point out that I'm the biggest sceptic around here, regarding Carol's weird capabilities. So far, I can't deny that she has come up with the goods. We'll know more by the end of the day, I'm sure. Right now, I'm willing to trust what she is relaying to us. That's between the three of us, though. I have no intention of admitting to that publicly, which is why Lorne and I will be darting here, there, and everywhere today."

Sean nodded. "Very well. I'm glad to hear it. I'll let you get on then. Lorne, I'll catch up with you another time. It's nothing major. Good luck on your hunt today, ladies."

"Wonder what that was all about?" Katy asked Lorne once they were inside the car, en route to the hospital.

"Not sure. I'm chomping at the bit to find out. Damn, why did we have such a tight schedule to deal with today?" Lorne complained, her mind running through the scenarios she knew were high up on Sean's agenda.

"Will you promise to tell me as soon as he lets you know?"

Lorne cringed. "Umm… only if he doesn't order me not to say anything."

"That's fair enough. What's your gut instinct telling you? Is he staying or going, do you think?"

"You know Sean—he's hard to read at the best of times. Did you see that twinkle in his eye? Really, it could go either way. He's always been a bit of a tease."

"Nothing worse than your immediate superior officer being bloody difficult to read. It can be a great source of frustration."

"I assure you that's intentional on his part. He's always loved winding people up."

CHAPTER TEN

Lorne and Katy trotted through the hospital after the receptionist informed them where to find Chris Dilbert. They flashed their IDs at the uniformed officer guarding the suspect's private room.

"How is he?" Katy asked, peeping through the portal window.

"Put it this way—he complains more than my missus, and I think she holds the world record for that."

"Maybe the docs will sedate him again once we've questioned him."

"Here's hoping," the officer said with a nod.

Dilbert eyed them with contempt when they entered his room.

A petite blonde nurse was in the process of checking his blood pressure. She looked up and smiled at them. "Are you family?"

Katy displayed her warrant card a second time. "Inspector Foster from the Met police. We're here to question the suspect. Is he up to that?"

"Yes, Mr. Dilbert is recovering well," the nurse replied.

Dilbert shot her an evil laugh, and her cheeks coloured up.

"I'll leave you to it. Press the buzzer if you need any assistance, Chris," she told the patient before packing up her equipment and moving towards the door.

Chris Dilbert watched the nurse intently, and just before she reached the door, he lifted the buzzer and pressed it.

The nurse paused. "Yes, Chris?"

"I *need* you to get rid of these women. I *need* rest."

Lorne opened the door for the nurse. "And we *need* to question the suspect about the disappearance and possible murder of an innocent woman. He's safe in our hands, nurse."

The nurse momentarily glared at Dilbert then hurried out of the room.

"Nice try, Dilbert. Look, the quicker you answer our questions, the sooner you can get on with your recuperation. If you're innocent, you've got nothing to worry about."

"I *am* innocent."

"Well, our records show that you're not averse to stalking or attacking women, so excuse us for putting you in the limelight as our prime suspect."

"What's this about?"

"An incident that you were involved in a few months back—six months ago, to be precise," Katy said, taking a step closer to the bed.

The man shuffled backwards to the edge of his bed and snarled. "What the hell are you talking about? I can't even remember what I had for effing breakfast on Friday last week. How are you expecting me to remember something which I'm supposed to have done six months ago?"

"Oh, you were definitely at the scene and tangled up in the incident. We have proof of that from more than one witness."

He sat forward in his bed. "What am I supposed to have done?"

"Do you frequent the Tickle Club?"

"Yep! What's that got to do with anything?"

Katy sighed. "A lot."

"You dissed me to that nurse. Said something about a murder. I ain't done nothing like that."

"Like I said, we have proof to the contrary. Let me refresh your memory of the incident. The night Noelle Chesterfield was dancing on her final shift at the club."

The suspect's frown deepened.

Katy continued, "Do you remember the girl in question, Mr. Dilbert?"

"Yeah, I remember her."

"Good, that makes our job easier. That night you and two other men confronted Noelle on the stage. Do you remember doing that?"

"Yeah. What's wrong with that?"

"Apart from being against the club's rules, you mean?"

Dilbert averted his gaze and grunted. "'Rules are there to be broken,' my pa always told me."

"Looks like listening to your pa's advice has dropped you in a pile of shit then, doesn't it?" Katy snapped back.

"I ain't done nothin' other than getting on that stage to get a close-up of the girl shaking her bits," Dilbert objected passionately.

Lorne snorted. "A case of bad eyesight, eh?"

"If you like. Jesus, ladies, give a man a break, will ya? If a girl wiggles her butt in my face, giving me the come-on, what am I going to do? Ignore it?"

"You're pathetic! The girl was doing her job, not giving you the come-on." Katy let out an extended sigh.

"You didn't see her. That night, she was definitely giving me the come-on. I swear, it's the truth."

"Had you seen Noelle dance on other nights at the club?"

Dilbert nodded. "Yeah, loads of times. That night, she was definitely acting differently."

Lorne and Katy glanced at each other with raised eyebrows.

"How many times have you seen Noelle dance at the club?" Katy asked.

"Dozens of times. Hey, I wasn't the only one who ran onto the stage that night, remember? The other guys must have picked up something strange about her performance that night, too, yes?"

"Maybe, maybe not. When we questioned the other two men, they didn't mention anything about Noelle acting differently. Are you sure her come-on wasn't in your twisted mind?" Katy prodded her finger in his temple.

He swiped her hand away as if she were an annoying wasp buzzing around his head before it struck. "Back off, lady. You lay another finger on me, and I'll sue you for assault. Got that?"

"You think that sort of language is what a totally innocent man should be using?"

"Whatever. I get the impression because of what's gone on in my past, that no matter how much I say I'm innocent, you ain't gonna believe me. Hey…" He pointed at Katy. "You told the nurse the girl was murdered. Is she dead?"

"As far as we know, yes, but you already know that. Don't you, Chris? Come on, be honest with us."

"Like shit I do. This is all news to me. I've visited the club several times since that night. If I had done anything to that bitch, do ya think I'd go back there?"

"Don't call her a bitch—not in my presence. Got that?" Katy shouted at him. "Respect the dead. All right?"

"All right, no need for you to get your knickers all twisted up. I repeat, I'm innocent. That night I did nothing but run on the stage. The security guys threw me out not long after."

"And you hung around outside, waiting for Noelle to finish her shift, yes?"

"No! I left the club and went straight home."

"And you have witnesses who can corroborate your alibi, of course?"

His eyes widened in fear. "No, of course I ain't."

"Then we have a problem, a very large problem that is leading us to think of you as our main suspect in Ms. Chesterfield's disappearance."

"No way! No effing way am I taking the rap for something I ain't done. No *way!*" he shouted. His clenched fists thumped the bed on either side of him.

Katy continued to grind the suspect, or try to, for the next twenty minutes, but after his petulant display, Dilbert refused to say anything further without a solicitor present. In the end, Katy said, "Okay, I can see we're wasting our time now. We'll leave you a few days to recover from your injury. An officer will remain outside your room at all times, just in case you get any ideas about taking off again. Once you're fit and well enough, we'll question you more at the station. You can have a solicitor present, and we'll take a DNA sample from you then, too. It will also give you a few days to reflect whether you should help us or not, Mr. Dilbert. Because one way or another, we're going to find out what happened to this young lady."

"Whatever," Dilbert said for the final time.

Lorne and Katy left the room.

"I want a twenty-four-hour watch on this man, no excuses, okay?" Katy said to the constable on guard.

"Yes, ma'am. Will you contact the station and inform them?"

"Right away. Don't let me down," Katy warned the police constable.

"You have my word."

With disappointment lingering in every step they took, they left the hospital and got back in the car in silence.

"What the heck are we going to do now?" Katy slipped the key into the ignition and hit the steering wheel with the palm of her hand.

"I hate to say it, but we need to focus on the information Noelle has fed us through Carol. Don't get despondent about Dilbert—he isn't going anywhere in the next few days. We can revisit and question him then. In the meantime, we have other leads to follow up. Keep positive and open to the unknown."

"At this stage, what other options are there left open to us? Right, give me a location to aim for."

Lorne opened her notebook and picked out one of the locations within an easy drive of their current position. "Okay, let's try this." She punched the address into Katy's sat nav.

Katy headed out of the car park and followed the woman's voice on the three-mile journey, dodging a traffic jam by dipping down a side street. Finally, the car drew up at one of the sites Tony and Lorne had pinpointed on the map the previous evening. Katy and Lorne got out of the car in the empty car park.

Lorne shuddered.

"What's wrong?"

She cast an eye over the area and shuddered again. "I'm not sure if it's the weather or something far more sinister at play right now. Maybe some of Carol's psychic powers have rubbed off on me during the haunting experience last night."

"Don't be so silly. It takes years to tune into a spirit's vibe."

Lorne tilted her head. "You seem to know an awful lot about a subject that doesn't hold any interest for you."

"I remember reading something like that in a magazine once, that's all."

"What, *Spooks* magazine?"

"Now you're just being ridiculous, woman, not forgetting guilty of wasting our time. Come on, buck your ideas up, and yes, that's an order."

Lorne pulled a face at her partner. "Nice to know I can rely on you for a dose of sympathy when needed."

Katy bared her teeth in a wide grin. They walked through the entrance along the wooded path and searched the area for nearly fifteen minutes. Disappointingly, they recognised only two of the clues Noelle had hinted at: a slight hill and a small bridge. So they decided to move onto the next area, where a similar result greeted them.

Lorne held her arms out to the side then slapped them against her thighs. "Crap! Nothing. So much for my creepy feeling."

"Let's not be so defeatist about this, Lorne. We've still got one area to look into. To me, it's the most likely area, too."

"Okay, we better get a move on then. It'll be getting dark soon."

"You're right." Katy opened the car door and jumped in behind the steering wheel. "I'm conscious of the timescale we're working with, but the fading light could hamper our search. Okay then. I think we should carry out the search in daylight tomorrow morning. How's that?"

Lorne tried not to react openly, but she failed miserably when a large breath left her body. "Works for me. Hey, maybe Carol will be able to give us some more clues before then."

"Perhaps. Are you going to call in and see her again after work?"

Lorne tried not to show her apprehension, but the shudder winding through her spine had other ideas. "I wasn't planning on putting myself in that situation two nights on the trot. Still, I will if you insist on me dropping over there."

"Let's weigh up the pros and cons."

Lorne had an inkling that Katy was about to force her to call in on her psychic friend on the way home whether she liked it or not.

Two miles from Carol's house, Lorne's mobile rang. Pulling into the side of the road, she answered the call. "Hello, Carol. Is that you?"

"It is, my dear. I wondered if you could spare me… er, I mean us, a few minutes before you head home?"

"Uh oh! I'm not liking the sound of the 'us' part."

"No need to be scared, Lorne. You know I'd never put you in any unnecessary danger."

"Okay, I was on my way over to see you anyway. Put the kettle on. I'll be about five minutes."

"Marvellous news."

Lorne spent the rest of the journey trying to soothe her nerves, but her previous night's experience prodded unrelentingly at her temple. "Shit. I hope I can cope with this," she grumbled as she trotted up the path to Carol's home.

Again, the living room was lit by eerie candlelight. Carol had left the front door on the latch for Lorne. Anxiously, she tiptoed through the house and lightly tapped her knuckles on the lounge door.

"Come in, Lorne. We've been expecting you."

Lorne anxiously glanced around the room, looking for the dim light she'd witnessed the previous evening. Carol patted the seat of the chair sitting alongside her. "Come, sit here next to me."

Reluctantly, Lorne let her feet guide her to the table. She plonked down into the chair, and immediately, an emerging light in the corner of the room drew her gaze.

"Come closer, child. You remember my dear friend, Lorne, don't you?" Carol reassured the spirit and rested her hand on top of Lorne's to put her at ease.

"Yes. She's trying to help me." The spirit's voice sounded a long way off in the distance.

Lorne tried not to let the incident affect her the way it had during their last meeting. "Hello, Noelle. Yes, I'm the policewoman dealing with your case."

Carol smiled and nodded at Lorne. "Noelle and I have been trying to search for new clues to assist you, Lorne, and we think we may have found one or two."

Her interest piqued, Lorne sat forward in her chair and clasped Carol's hand within her own. "Really? That would be very encouraging if you had."

"Before you got here, Noelle mentioned something that struck her. A tattoo of sorts. That's all we've managed to establish so far. Well, that and what Noelle perceived to be a garage."

"Hmm... that's interesting. The tattoo I have an idea about. I don't want to say more in case I influence what either you or Noelle has to say. However, the garage is flummoxing me, or is it?" Then Lorne recalled the problems they'd had with Simms. *The garage owner!* She continued, "One thing I forgot to mention to Noelle last night was the fact that we found her car."

A gasp wafted across the room and made the hairs on the back of Lorne's neck stand to attention. The dull light moved towards them. Lorne closed her eyes, urging herself to remain calm.

"That's excellent news. Isn't it, Noelle?" Carol asked, one eyebrow rising into her fringe.

"Yes and no. The forensics team is going over it now, searching for clues," Lorne said.

Carol tilted her head and asked, "Where did you find it, Lorne? Or am I not allowed to ask?"

"Don't be daft. Of course I can tell you. When the show aired the other night, we received a call from a scrapyard owner who recognised the car. Katy and I went to see the man, and *voila* there it was. The scrapyard owner even told us that a man with a distinctive tattoo dropped the car off on the back of a car loader."

"That's brilliant news. So he would have the man's name and address then, I'm assuming?"

"He did, yes. I'm sorry it turned out to be a dud one."

"Oh, nooooo!" Noelle wailed pitifully. The peculiar sound set Lorne's nerves jangling.

"Stay strong, Noelle. Forensics will find the clues we need, I assure you. In the meantime, when I left here last night, Tony and I examined the map searching for places that matched up to the clues you gave me. We found three possible locations. Katy and I visited two of these places today and found nothing. We decided to investigate the most likely place tomorrow, during the daylight. So we'll be going back there in the morning."

Carol's eyes narrowed as she absorbed the information. "Room for a little one on this excursion of yours?"

"You want to tag along?" Lorne asked, surprised.

"That was the plan, yes."

"I'd have to check with Katy first, but as far as I'm concerned, I think you coming with us to the scene would make perfect sense."

A sound like a round of applause filled the room. "Is that you agreeing with this scenario, Noelle?"

"Yes, it's an excellent idea for all of us to go there."

"Really? You'd do that for us? You'd guide us?" Lorne asked, flabbergasted.

"Yes. The clues are getting more pronounced. Where once upon a time I had doubts, now I am beginning to see things far more clearly."

Lorne hesitated briefly before voicing her next question. "Are things clear enough for you to tell me the name of your attacker yet?"

Noelle sighed. "No. Not yet."

Carol intervened, "Let's continue to let things flow, not try to push the information too much, for now anyway."

"Good idea. Although we have promised Noelle's parents a swift conclusion to the case."

Another sharp gasp came from the spirit's direction. "My parents!"

"Yes, Noelle. They're doing their best to remain positive. We all are. We're so dreadfully sorry the original police officers in charge of the case messed up. Katy and I are pulling out all the stops to put things right. Katy even promised your parents that we'd get things wrapped up by the end of the week. With your help, we could do that, couldn't we?"

Carol withdrew her hand from Lorne's and threw it out in the direction of the spirit. She smiled when they saw the light drift towards Carol. Lorne saw a faint outline of the spirit standing alongside her friend, and a feeling of elation tickled her spine when Carol said, "With the A-Team poised and ready for action, we will do our best to make sure Katy's promise is fulfilled." Turning to face the spirit, Carol whispered, "The day has come, sweetheart. It's what we've been looking forward to for days. Your death will be avenged with all of us girls working alongside you to achieve it."

"Let's hope so, Carol. Can I ring Katy now?" Lorne asked.

"Of course you can."

Lorne went into the hallway, leaving the door ajar. "Katy, it's me. Will you promise to hear me out? Okay. I'm at Carol's right now. We're not alone... Noelle is here with us. Look, I've told them about us taking a trip to the wooded area site, and well..."

Katy gasped. "No way! You can't ask me to go along with this, Lorne. You just can't."

"Why not? It makes perfect sense, Katy. We're crying out for guidance on this issue, and we have two people..." Lorne paused for a second, considering her words. "We have two *people* putting their all into this case. The least we can do is share this experience with them. What do you say?"

"Go on, Katy. What are you afraid of?" Carol called out, stifling a laugh.

"Cheeky mare! Tell her I'm afraid of suffering the wrath of the chief and the super when word of this gets out."

Lorne relayed the message, and Carol shouted back, "Excuses, excuses, Katy. Grow a pair, girl, and quickly. Remember that deadline you've inflicted upon yourself."

"Have you got this call on speaker phone, Lorne Warner?" Katy demanded.

"Nope. Come on, what have we got to lose? It's a win-win situation to me."

"Oh my Lord, I can't believe I—of sound mind and body—am about to agree to this absurd idea. I can just imagine it now when I go up for my achievement award. 'Ms. Foster, please let us in on your little secret of how you managed to wrap up a six-month cold case in only five days.' Holy crap, can you *imagine* what they'd say if I divulge that a psychic and a spirit solved the case, *not* my experienced partner and myself?"

"Yes! That's excellent news." Lorne pushed the door open, raised her thumb at Carol and Noelle, then joked, "Hey, those achievement awards are totally overrated. I bet if you looked back at the people who have received the awards, you'll find a load of bent coppers on the list. I'll even go as far to say that I bet Travers's and Campbell's names are on a list or two."

"Yeah, yeah. Ever the one with a smart-arse quick retort. Do you want to go directly to the site in the morning?"

"That makes sense to me. What time shall we meet up?"

"Nine o'clock on the dot. No slacking, sergeant. You hear me?"

"Yes, boss. Have a good evening."

"Huh! I'm sure to now, thanks to you sharing the news that I'm about to be guided by a spirit, in the flesh, so to speak."

Lorne laughed, hung up, and returned to the room. "She said she's looking forward to seeing you again tomorrow, Carol."

Carol sniggered. "I bet she is."

"If Noelle can't tell me anything else, I better make a move and get home to my family. Do you want me to pick you up in the morning, or will you follow me in your car?"

"We'll tag along behind you. If that's okay?"

"Sure, I'll be here at eight thirty then. Have a good evening. Try and get some rest." Lorne glanced over to the corner at the dull light. "Make sure you rest well, too, Noelle. Tomorrow is going to be a big day."

The light flickered several times and then disappeared.

"Is she all right, do you think?"

"Don't worry. We'll guide her through this. I suspect tonight will be a restless time for her, knowing that we're so close. If—and it's a big if—the area turns out to be where her life was taken."

"I never really thought about that. Let's hope, for her sake and ours, that turns out to be true. I'll see you bright and early in the morning then."

Carol walked Lorne to the door and kissed her on the cheek. "How's Tony's case coming along? Did you pass on the message about it not being what it seems?"

"Damn, I forgot to tell him."

"I wonder why that was. You must learn to control the amount you drink, Lorne, especially when you're in the middle of an important case such as this."

"Thank you, Carol. I feel suitably chastised and will make amends as soon as I get home this evening."

The second she stepped through the back door, Lorne blurted out what Carol had said regarding her husband's case. "It's not what it seems."

Charlie and Tony looked at her as if she'd just escaped from the local asylum.

"Excuse me?" Tony crossed the room and hugged her. "Have you had a stressful day, love?"

She laughed. "Sort of. I just dropped in to see Carol, and she urged me to tell you, 'It's not what it seems.' Thought I better say it as soon as I walked in as I forgot to tell you the other night, and she just emphasised the importance of you knowing that fact about your case."

"Well, that's interesting." Tony squeezed Lorne.

She tilted her chin and frowned. "Why?"

"At the end of our shift today, Joe and I effectively got the boot."

Lorne put her hands on his chest and pushed away from him. "He *sacked* you?"

"Yep. Pretty strange, huh?"

"Have you found anything that should question his decision?"

"No. The woman goes to work and carries out her job every day. Nothing suspicious at all from what we've witnessed."

She narrowed her eyes. "What are you going to do then?"

"I know that look. Why don't you tell me what you would do if you were in my shoes?"

"I'd revisit why the man employed you in the first place."

"And? If the guy no longer wants to employ us, we can't force him."

"I know that. Aren't you even slightly curious?"

"Of course I am. But Joe and I are of the same opinion—we can't do anything else for the man anyway."

"So you're just going to walk away?"

"No, we're going to look around for a new case where the person employing us is going to hopefully pay us some fees. I know what you're getting at, wifey dearest, and I'm not about to continue with a case that isn't going to pay to put food on our table. You might have done that once or twice in the past when you were running this business, but I have no intention of going down that route."

"Don't get angry with me. Don't Carol's words of wisdom mean anything to you?"

"Not really. I put up with that mumbo jumbo for your sake. Unlike you, I'd never use what she tells me to solve a case."

Lorne moved away from him and sat at the kitchen table. Henry rested his head on her lap to say hello. Petting the dog, she replied, "Are you reprimanding me, Tony, in a round-about way?"

"No. Yes. Oh, I don't know. I do think you're putting too much focus on where Carol is leading you." He sat in the chair next to her and gathered her hands in his. "I'm sorry if that's not what you want to hear, love. It's how I feel."

Charlie, who'd been quietly watching the interaction with a semi-open mouth, stood up and gently pushed her chair under the table.

"Everything all right, Charlie?" Lorne asked, concern tugging her heartstrings.

"I'm all right, Mum. You know how I feel about confrontations."

After exchanging guilty looks with her husband, Lorne jumped out of her chair to hug her daughter. "We're not confronting each other, sweetie. We're having a grown-up discussion. Please don't think it's anything more than that, Charlie. We wouldn't do that to you. Would we, Tony?"

"Of course not. Honestly, Charlie, your mother and I are bound to have a difference of opinion now and again. It's only natural. It doesn't mean that we're on the verge of falling out of love. She wouldn't let me for one thing." He winked.

"I'm glad to hear it. You guys are the perfect match, and I'd be mortified if you started having marriage problems. Maybe I'm feeling a little sensitive right now. I'll leave you to it."

"Hey, you can't drop that bombshell on us and run up to your room. What's going on, Charlie?"

"Nothing. Except Dad's just split up with his latest girlfriend. Nothing new there, right? It's fine, Mum. I just don't want you guys to end up the same way."

Lorne threw her arms around her daughter. "Tony and I would never split up. You have our word on that. We're more solid than the icebergs of the Arctic."

Lorne winced when Charlie tutted and shook her head.

"Not the best of analogies, Mum, considering how fast they're melting due to climate change."

Lorne waved the idea away. "Whatever, you know what I'm getting at. Now, get those silly thoughts out of your head."

"Okay. I'm still going to let you guys get on with your conversation. I made a spag bol. You just need to heat it through and boil the spaghetti. Call me when it's ready."

Lorne shook her head and watched her daughter leave the room. "Thanks, Charlie. You're an absolute angel," she called after her.

"Yeah, I know," Charlie shouted back, running up the stairs.

Lorne clutched Tony's hand. "We are all right, aren't we?"

Tony shook his head in despair. "Of course we are. Let's agree to disagree on the Carol angle, shall we?"

"Okay. But saying that… maybe you should keep an eye on your client just for one more day. Go on, just to please me?"

He held his arms out to the side. "All right, if it means getting some peace and quiet around here. Not sure what Joe will think about the prospect of turning out for another boring shift of wife-watching, without getting paid. I do think there's something strange about this situation that I'm having trouble pinpointing."

"In that case, take care. We both know how many nutters there are around nowadays."

"Don't worry about me. You're the one who needs to take care."

Lorne kissed him and smiled. "I've got it covered, agent boy. Hey, I haven't called you that in a long time."

"No, thank goodness," Tony groaned light-heartedly.

CHAPTER ELEVEN

After a restless night of anticipating what the new day would have in store for them, Lorne showered, dressed then grabbed a quick coffee and a piece of toast. She rushed out of the house at eight twenty. The first car to join the convoy was Carol's reliable mini. They drove to the scene and met up with Katy, who was waiting for them inside her car with her heater on full blast and her music blaring.

Lorne banged on the windscreen to get her partner's attention.

Katy clutched her chest in fright. "Jesus, you scared the crap out of me."

"I thought detectives remained alert at all times." Lorne grinned broadly.

Katy hopped out of the car and shook hands with Carol. "Good to see you again, Carol. I hope this experience doesn't freak me out too much. Forgive me if my attention wavers now and again and I stick to the traditional route of investigating, won't you?"

"You do whatever you feel comfortable with, Katy. It might take me a while to summon up Noelle's spirit anyway."

"Oh," Katy said, sounding surprised. "Noelle didn't hitch a ride with you in the car then?"

"No, Katy. You really haven't grasped how the spirit world works. You carry on. I'll lag behind and do what I usually do to call on the spirits for their guidance."

"All right then, let's get this show on the road. Shall we set off in this direction?"

Lorne stopped at the edge of the wood to read the instructions of where the trail might lead them. "Okay, this is interesting. Apparently, this area was used by the druids for all kinds of ceremonies years ago."

"Well, that snippet of information might mean that we're confronted with other spirits once we're inside the forest. I hope not. And I'll do my best to keep the spirits from interfering with our quest, but if they are resident here, that might prove to be an impossible task," Carol explained.

"Wow, really? The spirits claim certain areas as their own? I never imagined them doing that," Katy admitted.

The two detectives started to wind their way along the path, through the canopied area, which was littered with autumn leaves in every shade of rust imaginable. Now and then, they halted to watch Carol trying to summon Noelle, only to fail. They continued on the same route, scanning their surroundings for any of the clues that had designated this stretch of the county as a place of interest.

Stopping, her feet buried in damp leaves, Lorne pointed through the haze the chilly morning had mustered, indicating a collection of stones alongside the path. "Is that what we're looking for?"

Katy took a few steps closer and called back over her shoulder. "If I'm not mistaken, it's a bridge of sorts. Not sure it leads anywhere, though."

The three of them moved closer to the stones. "You're right. It used to be a bridge at one time. Looks like it's been dismantled." Lorne kicked the twigs and leaves away from the base of the stones.

"Can you tell us anything about this, Carol?"

"Not much. Yes, it was a bridge." She shuddered.

Lorne and Katy glanced at each other and frowned.

"Everything all right, Carol?" Katy asked. She stepped forward and rubbed the psychic's upper arm.

"There are so many here."

"Spirits?" Katy looked more frightened than Lorne had ever seen her before, which surprised Lorne, given the way Katy had reacted the previous day at a similar location.

"Yes." Carol went into a kind of trance.

Lorne moved behind her friend in case she lost her balance. Contacting the spirits often drained Carol's energy.

"Many people have been killed here."

"No!" Katy cried out, horrified. She leapt closer to Lorne and clung to her arm.

"Don't worry. They won't harm you," Carol reassured the detectives. "Once this is over, I need to return to free these poor people from their state of limbo. Maybe there will be a few more cold cases for you to solve in this vicinity. Noelle, are you with us, dear?"

Lorne stifled a snigger when she felt Katy's grip tighten on her arm. Katy's head swivelled like a deranged bird's as she searched their surroundings.

"Chill. If she appears, you'll be fine. Take deep breaths. Carol won't let anything happen to us."

Carol turned to face Katy, placed a hand on her forehead, and mumbled a few words.

"What's she doing?" Katy mouthed.

"I'm protecting you. Just breathe deeply, and you'll be fine."

Lorne couldn't help but be impressed by the immediate transformation in Katy's demeanour once Carol had removed her hand.

"Do you feel different?" Lorne asked.

"Actually, I do. It's hard to describe how I feel. I suppose *calmer* would be a good word."

"Come, ladies. We need to travel deeper into the depths of the wood." Carol took the lead.

Lorne and Katy linked arms and constantly surveyed the area behind her as they followed. Carol's black cloak separated the eerie mist floating inches above the forest floor. Lorne got the impression that if Carol hadn't performed the protection ceremony on Katy, she would have taken flight and locked herself in her car. As for Lorne, she was feeling pretty chilled, in more ways than one.

Twigs snapped at regular intervals beneath their feet, and the mixture of dry and moist leaves rustled, adding to their spooky surroundings as they ventured deeper into the wood. Carol stopped abruptly in front of them. Katy and Lorne continued a few steps and came to a halt beside her. They shuffled into a new position, standing with their backs against each other, in a circle, just listening.

"There." Lorne pointed a few feet away at a flickering faint light.

"That's it. Noelle, be with us. Show us the way, dear." Carol held her arms up to beckon the spirit.

Katy's eyes widened, and her gaze slipped between watching the spirit and Lorne. She seemed to be in shock, if only temporarily.

Lorne leaned over and whispered, "She's arrived. Stay calm. Everything will be fine."

Katy could only nod in response.

"Noelle, can you lead the way now? We'll follow wherever you want to take us."

"Okay. It's quite a distance from here, I think," the spirit replied, her faint image emerging.

Katy gasped. Noelle's distinctive shape, which Lorne hadn't been privy to previously, led the way.

Carol smiled at Lorne and Katy and punched the air. "Here we go, ladies. We should have this case sewn up by lunchtime if all goes well."

"Let's hope so," Katy mumbled, linking her arm through Lorne's.

Noelle's spirit chose a bush and circled it. "The beautiful tree I mentioned. I have no idea of the name."

Lorne nodded. "It's a rhododendron. It might not look much now. But back in May, when the incident occurred, it would have possibly been in full bloom. Was it, Noelle?"

"Yes. Beautiful, it has pale-pink flowers. Is it fair for such beauty to witness such a vile act of pure evil?" Noelle stated, ending her question with a sob.

"It's all right, Noelle. With your help, we'll see this person gets the punishment he rightly deserves. Keep strong and lead on, if you will, sweetie," Lorne assured the spirit. As they walked, she kept a mental note of the clues they had uncovered so far: the bridge and the beautiful 'tree'. Noelle had also mentioned gravestones.

Lorne wondered if Noelle had felt the presence of all the other spirits who had found this place as their final resting place. Perhaps the gravestones had not been exactly literal. Or were they about to stumble across an actual cemetery? Lorne tried to recall the map. However, the unfamiliar surroundings in conjunction with the cold morning air jumbled her head.

The three women continued to follow the spirit, who stopped now and again to take in her surroundings as if questioning the route she was taking, especially when a new path appeared. Once she took a specific route, Noelle seemed confident and never once turned back. Still, Katy clung to Lorne's arm, and Lorne suspected her boss was worried about what might happen to her if she let go.

At a large clearing, about ten minutes into their journey, Noelle stopped. She spun around, her arms out to the side as though she were in some kind of vortex, stirring up the leaves beneath her. "Here! This is where it happened."

"That's wonderful, Noelle." Carol applauded.

"Wow, really? Do you think that's right, Lorne?" Katy asked, unlinking her arm from Lorne's.

"Why should we doubt it, Katy, given the clues that she has verified on this outing so far? My heart's pounding with excitement. Isn't yours?"

"I'm not sure I'm as excited as you are about this, but my heart is certainly going ten to the dozen. So, what's next?"

"Let's see how things progress for a few more minutes. After that, I suppose we should call in forensics and the cadaver dogs, yes?" Lorne replied.

"Okay, you're right." Katy lowered her voice and said, "I hope Noelle decides to disappear again before anyone else arrives at the scene. I don't fancy explaining her presence to anyone else, and if word ever got back to either the chief or the super—let's just say if I'd been blessed with bollocks, they'd be extracted from between my legs and shoved down my throat."

Lorne sniggered and shook her head. "I think that's a slight exaggeration, but I do understand what you're getting at."

For the next few minutes, they watched and listened to Noelle, spinning on the spot and sobbing her heart out until exhaustion finally subdued her.

"Is she all right, Carol?" Lorne asked, watching Noelle fall in a heap on the damp forest floor.

"She'll be fine. It's relief, Lorne. She's done her job leading us here. Now it's down to you and Katy to find her body."

"We'll do our best. Katy and I are going to head back to the car. The reception for our phones is crap here. We'll contact the relevant departments to come out here. Do you want to head off home? Will Noelle disappear now, too?"

"Are you worried what the others might think if they turn up and see a psychic with the spirit of your missing victim in tow?"

Lorne hugged her friend. "You've got me bang to rights, love. Not that we don't appreciate your help."

"I understand completely. Can you wait a little while longer? I need to make sure Noelle is all right first before I send her away."

"Of course. It'll take us a good few minutes to get back to the car anyway. Will that be enough time?"

Carol glanced in the direction of the crumpled outline of the spirit and shrugged. "I think so. Who knows with these things? Let me check how she is."

Katy nudged Lorne's arm. "I hope they're not going to be too long. My feet are getting colder by the minute."

"Patience was never your strongest attribute, was it? They'll be as long as they need to be."

Before Lorne's eyes, the spirit evaporated. Carol rejoined Lorne and Katy, and together, they marched swiftly back through the wood to their vehicles.

Katy clapped her hands together. "Let's get this party started."

"Er... I think I would have said that a little differently under the circumstances, boss."

"I agree with Lorne. A little less enthusiasm and far more compassion for the victim should be the order of the day, Inspector."

"Oops, okay. You guys are right. I apologise wholeheartedly. You both must feel as elated as I'm feeling right now, though, right?"

"Maybe. Let's see what a search of the area shows up first before we begin our celebrations, eh?" Lorne said.

Carol nodded her agreement as Katy placed the calls.

Turning her back on Katy, Lorne asked her dear friend, "Will Noelle be released now? You know, be able to continue on her onward journey to the other side?"

"Not yet. Her body has to be discovered before that can occur. Let's hope the spot she pointed out is the correct area. I've never seen her react in such a distraught way during any of her visits. From that, I think we can presume that place has to have some significance."

"Hopefully, depending how soon the teams can get here, we'll have some answers by the end of the day."

"What if her body isn't here? What will happen then, Lorne?" Carol asked, her brow wrinkled.

"We'll cross that bridge when, or if, we come to it. Why don't you go home, get some rest in front of that warm wood-burning stove of yours?"

"I might just do that. You will ring me the minute you hear any news?"

"Of course I will. Thanks for all your help, Carol. It's been an amazing experience. Opened a few sceptics' eyes, too, I believe." Lorne nodded in Katy's direction, where she was in her element, issuing orders and giving the directions to their location.

"I'm glad we've achieved something today. I have a niggling feeling in the pit of my stomach causing me concerns."

"About the case? Whether or not we're going to find Noelle's remains here?"

"I can't tell you any more than that, Lorne. You know how these things work. We just have to go with the information these spirits bestow upon us. Fingers crossed. I'm out of here, Onyx missed her walk this morning."

"Give her a kiss from me. Drive carefully, and thanks again, Carol. I'll call you this evening if I hear anything."

CHAPTER TWELVE

When the forensics team arrived, Lorne felt as if they had taken an eternity to get to the scene, though they were the first to arrive.

"Geeze, guys, what kept you? It's been bloody hours since I placed the call," Katy complained as the two men in their thirties stood at the rear of their car, donning white suits.

"We got held up on another call. It's not like this is an emergency or anything, is it?" The sarcastic comment had come from the cutest of the men and was adjoined by the broadest of smiles.

"Less of the cheek and more urgency is needed, if you don't mind, Samuels. Have you seen how cold it is out here today?"

"Sorry, yep. I didn't take that into consideration. I forgot what wimps you detectives are."

Katy glanced at Lorne and raised an eyebrow. "Let's hope you're feeling this chirpy after you spend the next four hours out here."

"Touché, Inspector. Are you sticking around?"

"If you had been here a few hours ago, maybe. I think you can handle it from here while I thaw out. Will you ring me straight away if you find anything?" Katy handed him one of her business cards, which he tucked in the side of the bag he was holding.

"That's an affirmative. Now, if you'll excuse us, ladies, we have a crime scene to investigate."

"You can't get rid of us that quickly. We need to show you the way. Lorne, will you stay here and wait for the other team while I take these gentlemen in?"

"Sure. We wouldn't want the men to get lost, knowing what lies in this forest."

"Sounds ominous. Care to share what you're referring to by that?" Samuels frowned.

"It doesn't matter. Let's get a move on before the light starts to fade." The other forensic guy pulled Samuels by the arm and headed through the forest's entrance.

Katy grinned broadly and tapped her nose at the two men. "If you'd like to walk this way, gents."

Lorne jumped back in the car and switched the engine on to circulate the heat in the confined space. Some days, she really regretted returning to the Met—this was definitely one of those days.

She would much rather have been scooping up poop at the kennels than having every inch of her skin prickling with cold.

A car pulled into the car park. Lorne got out of the vehicle to welcome the police cadaver dog team, only to find it wasn't them. The man behind the steering wheel stared at her, his eyes wide with fear. *Well, he looks suspicious. Wonder what he's up to?*

She walked towards his car, and the engine roared to life. Lorne upped her speed. His wheels spun, churning up the car park's gravel. Some of it hurtled Lorne's way. She cried out as a huge piece clipped her shin.

"Stop! Police!"

The man put his foot down and exited the area like a Formula One racing driver.

"Stop!" Lorne repeated to no avail.

"Who was that?" Katy trotted up behind her.

"I'm not sure. Maybe he was about to dump something illegal. He saw me and got spooked. Excuse the turn of phrase."

"Did you get the number plate?"

Lorne took out her notebook and scribbled down the number. "I certainly did. I'll run it through the system when we get back to base, see what comes up."

"No sign of the dog team yet, I take it?" Katy asked, rubbing her hands together.

"Nope. Oh, hang on. Here they are now." Lorne pointed at the white van pulling into the end of the road.

"Good. I'm freezing my tits off out here. Let's get back to the station and run that plate. I hope this buoyant mood I'm in doesn't disappear into the ether like Noelle's spirit."

Upon arrival at the station, the first thing they did was to grab a hot coffee and a sausage roll to make up for the lunch they had missed. Lorne asked Karen to run the strange car's plate number through the system. Lorne was at the whiteboard, filling in details they had discovered that morning, when Karen excitedly called over to her.

"Lorne, the car is registered to… you're never going to believe this…"

"Go on, surprise me. It's the bloody boyfriend, yes?"

"Yep," Karen agreed with a grimace.

Lorne kicked out at the nearest table leg. "Shit! I should have known it was him just by the way he reacted."

Katy came out of her office when she heard the commotion. "Something wrong?"

"I had him in the palm of my hand and let him go—that's what's wrong."

"Who? Lorne, you're not making any sense."

"Smalling. Noelle's boyfriend. That was him earlier."

"Crap. All right. There's no point beating yourself up. Karen, have you got an address for him?"

"I have indeed." Karen handed the details to Katy as she passed.

Katy joined Lorne at the board. "Okay, I'll ask the obvious question. Why, after six months, do you think he returned to the scene?"

Lorne leaned in so the rest of the team couldn't hear. "Maybe Noelle worked her magic."

"What's that supposed to mean?"

Lorne tutted. "Perhaps her spirit in some way affected his conscience."

Katy pulled back and stared at her. "Lorne, over the years you've said some bizarre things, but that has to be the craziest."

It was Lorne's turn to be surprised. "What? How can you question what I'm saying after what we both witnessed this morning?"

"Easily. It just doesn't add up." Katy raised a finger and, in slow motion, pointed out a word on the whiteboard. She circled it with her finger. "There you go. Nothing suspicious about it. Pure fact."

"*Crimewatch?*" Lorne's mouth twisted as she thought over her partner's suggestion. "What? You think he saw the show the other night, and it pricked his guilty conscience into turning up there today?"

"Why not?" Katy folded her arms and tapped her foot.

"Because if that were to happen logically, wouldn't he have shown up at the scene the following day, you know, the day after the reconstruction aired? That was three days ago, wasn't it? I'm not saying you're wrong by any means. However, I do think the timing is off by more than a little."

"Maybe this was the first opportunity he's had since the show aired. I don't know—I'm surmising that's what has taken place. We won't know for sure until we bring him in for questioning, *if* we can track the bugger down. My take is he'll go underground again after almost being caught."

Lorne kicked the table leg again. "Damn! Why wasn't I quicker to react?"

"Stop it, woman. It's about time we started thinking about the positives to the case and not the negatives. Things are certainly looking up from where I'm standing."

Lorne pulled a face. "I would hold back on ringing the parents with any good news just yet, until they uncover Noelle's body."

"I have no intention of ringing them until the end of the week. Fancy a trip out to see if we can track down Smalling?"

Lorne heaved a long sigh. "To be honest, I'm chilled to the bone and would find it hard to accept another disappointment today. Why don't you send Graham and Stephen after him?"

"This isn't like you, Lorne. What's really going on?"

Lorne shrugged. "If I could tell you, I would. I've just got such a negative vibe running through me at the moment, I have a feeling it's going to be difficult to shake off. Maybe I just need to warm up first."

"All right. I'll accept your rejection this once. Never again, though. Got that?" Katy retorted more sternly than Lorne had anticipated.

She kicked herself for the way she was reacting. It was totally out of character for her, and she found the feeling very unsettling. Maybe her experience with Noelle's spirit was having more effect on her than she'd realised. Katy drifted away and left Lorne staring at the information on the board. She picked up the marker pen and wrote: "Possible burial site found for Noelle Chesterfield." Then she returned to her desk and rang the forensics lab to see if there was any news regarding the DNA samples from Noelle's car and handbag. The negative response only added to her despondent mood.

Lorne, Katy, and the team spent the rest of the afternoon checking and rechecking the information they had gathered so far. Finally, the call they'd been waiting for came in at around five thirty. Katy took the call, but Lorne could tell the news wasn't good. Lorne's gut feeling was apparently still in full working order.

Katy hung up and called the team to attention. "Listen up, people. Our job is far from over on this case. The site turned out to be a false alarm. After extensive digging by the two teams at the site, they've managed to find nothing linking it to Noelle Chesterfield."

"Crap. I had a feeling the results would come back negative," Lorne grumbled.

Katy shrugged. "Well, we did our best. We just have to hope that Stephen and Graham come up with the goods. If not, we've got no other option except to put this down as another wasted day. I'm really not sure how many more of those we can take. Okay, let's wind things up for the evening, folks. Go home, get some rest, and start anew in the morning."

To compound everyone's negativity, Stephen and Graham entered the incident room.

Graham shook his head. "Nothing. Sorry, boss."

"What? He wasn't there? Or he doesn't live at that address?" Katy queried.

"He lives there, all right. The thing is, none of his neighbours have seen him at the property lately," Graham replied, dropping his weary frame into the chair at his desk.

Katy puffed out her cheeks and slapped her hands against her thighs. "Could this day really get any bloody worse? Where's he hiding out? We'll look into that in the morning. Okay, let's call it a day, peeps."

Chairs scraped on the floor, and the sound of computers being put into hibernation filled the incident room. With slouched shoulders, Lorne left the station.

When she arrived home, she found Charlie sitting at the kitchen table, talking on the phone. "Hold on, Carol. She's just walked in now."

Lorne waved her hands and shook her head. It proved to be pointless, though.

Charlie urged her to take the phone she was thrusting at her.

"Thanks, Charlie." She tried to sound chirpier than she felt when she spoke to Carol, "Hi, Carol. How are things?"

"Less of the small talk, Lorne. I can sense when something is wrong."

Lorne eased herself into the chair and petted Henry on the head. "Not good news, I'm afraid, sweetie. Looks like our little adventure this morning was for nothing. The teams haven't found anything relating to Noelle at all. No clues and certainly no sign of her body. Is there any way Noelle might have taken us to the wrong place?"

"Nope. She was adamant about that. Crikey, I don't believe it. You saw her reactions at that place. She was more animated than

I've ever seen her before. It's incredible they haven't found anything."

"Yep, especially considering what occurred after you left the scene." Lorne cringed, wishing she hadn't opened her mouth.

"Go on. What happened? You're going to have to tell me now, Lorne."

Under Charlie's watchful eye, Lorne admitted, "We have reason to believe that Noelle's boyfriend pulled up at the location."

Charlie sat bolt upright in her chair. Her eyes nearly popped out of her head.

Lorne nodded.

"Really? Did you speak to him?" Carol asked, sounding surprised by the revelation.

"Hardly. He drove into the car park and was acting suspiciously, so I approached the car. He took off before I could talk to him."

"Well, that is odd. Don't you think?"

"It is. One piece of good news is that we traced his number plate and discovered his address."

"I sense a *but* coming soon," Carol said.

"Yeah, we sent a couple of officers out to the address, but the neighbours said they hadn't seen him for months."

"Okay, let me see what I can do this evening. I'm dying to ask what the gentleman's name is, but don't tell me. Maybe Noelle will pay me a visit this evening. My thoughts are that she'll be too exhausted to show up. Fingers crossed, eh?"

"I seem to be doing that a lot lately with this one. I better go and throw some dinner together before Tony gets home. I'll call you tomorrow, Carol. Good luck."

"Thanks. Hey, at least one of us has had a good day today. Be proud of your hubby, Lorne. That's all I'm prepared to say."

"Wait! You can't leave me up in the air like that, you tease!"

Carol laughed. "Can't I?"

"All right, speak soon." Lorne disconnected the call and glared at her daughter. "Thanks for the support. I'll think carefully the next time you want your arse covered, young lady."

"Whatever, Mum. I could hear the desperation in Carol's voice. You would have done the same in my position."

"Probably. Has Tony rung?"

"Nope, not today. He should be home soon," Charlie said, rising from her chair and flicking the switch on the kettle.

Lorne and Katy almost jumped out of their skins when the back door flew open and Tony marched in.

He punched the air a few times and shouted, "Incredible! We knew there was something amiss with that guy. I'm so pleased you encouraged us to stick with him today. Bloody hell, the audacity of the bloke."

"Do we have to take it in turns, trying to guess what your client did? I take it that's who you're talking about?"

"Too right. I'll have a coffee, Charlie, if you don't mind. It's been a long day. Sorry to be so overexcited. How was your day, love?"

"Not half as exciting as yours, obviously. I insist, you go first."

Tony dropped into the chair next to hers and leaned over to kiss her cheek. "Well, this is how my day panned out. Did I mention that it was incredible?"

She chortled. "Yes, you did."

"Well, Joe and I turned up at the client's house this morning at eight thirty, as usual. His wife normally leaves for work around five minutes after we arrive. This morning, however, she didn't. There was no sign of either of them up until midday. So I persuaded Joe to stay at the house while I went to the wife's workplace. I thought it would be better to turn up in person rather than make a phone call to see if she was at work."

"And? Was she?" Lorne asked, her interest rising.

"Nope. There's a surprise, eh? She's as regular as clockwork. He fires us one day, and the very next day, her routine changes. Very dubious, eh?"

"Wow, so what did you do? Tackle him about it?"

"No. I returned to the car, and Joe and I decided to sit and observe the house for the rest of the day. We saw no evidence of anyone being inside the house until around five o'clock."

"Until dusk?"

"Yep, even then the house was only lit by a dull light. The front door opened, and out sneaks our client, looking very shifty. Thank goodness we had the foresight to change vehicles this morning. Anyway, we tailed him to some kind of storage area. There were row upon row of garages. Joe and I got out of the car and followed him on foot. He went inside one of the garages. We seized the opportunity to get closer."

Lorne eased forward to the edge of her chair. "Go on."

"He stayed inside the garage for around ten minutes, locked it up using a padlock, and left the area."

Lorne nodded excitedly. "Carol mentioned a garage, didn't she?"

"So she did. Maybe she was getting confused between the two cases."

"More than likely."

"When we thought the coast was clear, we ran up to the garage and listened for any possible noise coming from inside. Joe tapped on the door, and we heard something move inside."

"No! What was it? A person? Or an animal?"

"Patience, wifey dearest, I'm coming to that."

"I called out. At first, we heard nothing. Then I thought I heard a faint muffled noise. I asked Joe if he heard anything, but he hadn't caught it. It was barely audible, though. I knocked again, and, thankfully, Joe heard the response this time. He ran and grabbed a hacksaw from the car. When we finally opened the door, there was Mrs. Dixon, tape across her mouth, blindfolded, with rope tied around her ankles and wrists."

"Oh my God, that poor woman. Why?"

"Which was the first thing I asked her once I'd released her of her bindings. The poor woman was so shaken up, it took her ages to calm down enough to tell us."

"Did you take her to the police station?"

"Eventually, yes. Although I thought she should get checked out at the hospital first. She said apart from being shaken up, physically, she felt fine."

"So, what was his motivation?" Lorne asked, shaking her head in disgust. The woman could have died all manner of deaths in that space: hypothermia, suffocation, anything.

"He had accused her of having an affair. She knew that Joe and I had been employed to watch her every move, and she was appalled by his distrust and swore that she had never given him a reason to question her faithfulness."

"That's strange. What makes a person think like that without a genuine reason then?"

"She also said that he'd been under a lot of stress since losing his job. Even though she'd tried several times to persuade him to see the doctor for what she perceived to be depression, he refused. Instead, he turned the tables on her, got it into his head that she was trying to drive him mad, and decided to put a stop to it. Then she broke down in tears."

"Who can blame her? What a traumatic time for the poor woman. The man must be deemed criminally insane to do such a thing to his wife."

"You haven't heard the best part yet. Apparently, up until a few months ago—" Tony paused and reached for Lorne's hand. "They had a dog, which she idolised. One day, she came home from work and found the dog lying on the kitchen floor, having convulsions. She rushed it to the vet. Sadly, the poodle died before the vet had a chance to try and save it."

"Oh no, the poor thing. What on earth was wrong with it?"

"Mrs. Dixon said the vet told her the dog had been poisoned. At the time, she put it down to something the dog had picked up in the park on one of his walks. However, yesterday, before he trussed her up and shoved her in the garage, her husband admitted that he'd poisoned the dog himself."

"How dreadful. I'd like to get my hands on the bastard and shove some poison down his neck, see how he effing likes it."

"Yeah, I thought you'd say that. I felt the same way once I heard what he'd done. Sick shit! Anyway, Mrs. Dixon also told us that she was very relieved that we had discovered her before it was too late. When I asked her what she meant by that, apart from the obvious of course, she said that her husband had told her every detail about how he intended to end her life."

"Goodness me. Tony, before you go on, please tell me you've got the police to arrest this bastard?"

"No fear of that. We dropped Mrs. Dixon off at the police station and left her there to be seen by the police doctor while we accompanied a couple of officers back to the house to arrest him. He was absolutely livid, especially as we caught him in the act of gathering together all the torture instruments he could lay his hands on in his garage. He had saws, bolt cutters, rope, a blowtorch—you name it, he'd loaded it into a holdall, ready for the next day's activities."

"Jesus, and you thought the PI business was going to be boring!"

"Yeah, how wrong can a man be? Anyway, Mrs. Dixon said he'd taunted her, his face barely inches from hers, about where he intended to kill her."

Lorne gasped. "That's bloody torture in itself, doing that. Where?"

"He had hired a boat and was intending taking her aboard. He was going to take the boat out into the channel to give her a burial at sea—after he'd cut her up into tiny pieces. Then he was going to sail away and live it up on the life insurance money."

"Oh my goodness. The disgusting plans people create. He had it all figured out. Thank God you and Joe managed to prevent him carrying out his warped proposal, Tony." She leaned over and kissed his lips. "My hero."

His cheeks coloured up, and he waved his hand in front of him. "Stop it. If you hadn't pushed me into going back there today, this bastard would have carried out his intentions and probably got away with it. Maybe it was your gut instinct working its magic on my case. Talking of cases, how has yours progressed today?"

"Slowly. Actually, that's not quite true. This morning, everything looked hunky-dory, but our elation was doused with cold water this afternoon."

"I'm not with you. Start from the beginning."

By the end of Lorne's story, Tony was sitting in his chair, staring at her open-mouthed. "Damn, and there was me, thinking that my eventful day would top yours by a country mile. How wrong was I?"

"It's not a competition, love. It just shows what a crazy world we live in. Why on earth people insist on hurting each other is a constant cause of concern for me. Anyway, do you have any other jobs lined up?"

"Not yet, no. Not unless you need a helping hand tracking down your bastard, that is?" Tony winked at her.

"Hmm... you're not joking, either, are you? Well, I could have a word with Katy tomorrow if you like? She's made the mistake of telling the parents that she intends wrapping the case up by the end of the week; something I wouldn't have done when I was an inspector. The problem is, we've become reliant on a spirit to solve the case. You should have witnessed what Katy and I saw today, Tony. It was unbelievable."

"I'm sure it was. It's giving me the creeps just thinking about it. Look, I think working together is doable. But then, I don't want to put pressure on you. Have a talk to Katy and get back to me tomorrow. No offence taken if the answer is no, okay?"

They shook hands and left the table. "Help me organise dinner?" Lorne asked.

"Of course. What did you have in mind?"

"Charlie? What do you fancy for dinner?"

"Pizza, chips, and beans will do me, Mum."

Lorne smiled. "There we go—junk food it is then. You put the fryer on, and I'll start chopping up the onions and peppers to go on the top. They never put enough topping on for me."

Tony shook his head and mumbled, "No one is ever capable of doing things to your standard, Lorne. Ever."

"I'm glad you've finally realised that, love." She kissed him again then removed the ingredients she needed from the fridge and started to prepare them.

CHAPTER THIRTEEN

Lorne arrived at work the following morning, where the mood was mixed. Katy had arranged for all the patrol vehicles in the area to be on the lookout for Smalling's car. The result came back negative from the night shift.

Where are you, you bastard? And why did you show up at the scene out of the blue like that?

"Penny for them?" Katy said, winding her way through the desks towards the vending machine.

"Just thinking. Why do you suppose Smalling turned up like that yesterday?"

Katy shrugged and sipped her coffee. "Who knows? Would it be worth sending a uniform team out to the forest today to see if he shows up again?"

"To my mind, he's not likely to return there anytime soon."

"So, where does that leave us today then?" Katy asked.

"I don't know. Hey, you think our case is bad? You wait until I tell you what Tony went through yesterday with his."

"Grab a coffee and come into the office and tell me."

By the time Lorne had finished telling her partner the tale, Katy's eyes were protruding, making her look like one of the pop-eye fish Lorne's dad used to keep in his aquarium.

"Holy crap. It's a good job Tony took on board your suggestion of returning yesterday. Otherwise, the sneaky shit might have got away with killing his wife."

"Too right. Which brings me nicely to why I brought up the subject."

"Go on. Not that I don't know what's about to drop out of your mouth next."

"Huh, me predictable? That'll be the day. What if we get Tony and Joe to do some snooping for us?"

"Um… because we have a team of our own sitting out there, kind of twiddling their thumbs, and I'm including us in that scenario, too."

"I hear you, boss. It was just a thought," Lorne said, feeling a little dejected.

"No worries. Can you gather all the information that came in overnight regarding the case and give forensics another prod for me? Although I'm pretty sure we know who the assailant is already."

"Well, Noelle hasn't actually told us it was her ex yet, but I'll keep hounding forensics."

"Okay, leave me to deal with this lot, and I'll be with you in an hour or so."

Lorne left Katy to get on with wading through her pile of post and messages and went back to her desk. Around thirty minutes later, her phone rang. "Hello, DS Warner. How may I help?"

"I need to go back there. *We* need to go back there, Lorne."

She sighed. "As in right now, Carol? Can't this at least wait until this afternoon?"

"No. We need to get back there immediately. Noelle is driving me insane."

"In what way?"

"She's distraught because she's finally discovered who murdered her. Lorne, she knows it was her boyfriend. She's even named him— Danny Smalling."

"That's great news. Right name, too, although I can't see what the point of going back to the forest is, Carol. Forensics and the police cadaver dogs searched the area and found nothing. Even if I wanted to, I'm not sure I could persuade Katy to waste more time at the site."

"Well, that's a shame. I guess Noelle and I will have to venture over there by ourselves then. I'll let you know how we get on when I get back." Carol hung up.

Lorne went to Katy's office. "Can you talk for a second?"

"Sure, take a seat. I need a breather anyway. You look concerned. What's wrong?"

"I've just received a call from Carol."

"That sounds ominous."

"She informed me Noelle had given her Smalling's name and said that she wanted to go back to the forest."

Katy shook her head. "I'm not sure I could stand going on another wild-goose chase, Lorne. Could you?"

"No, and that's exactly what I told her."

"So, what's with the face?" Katy sat back in her chair and bounced a few times.

"Well, before she hung up on me, she told me that she and Noelle were on their way over there now."

"Crap. That's not what I wanted to hear. That dear friend of yours can be a pain in the butt sometimes."

"I thought the same. Do you think we should go out there, given that Smalling showed up at the spot yesterday?"

"It's a no-brainer." Katy bounced forward and slipped her jacket off the back of the chair. "Come on. We better get over there; see what the pair of them come up with this time. But we need emphasise to Carol that this is the last time we're going to the forest, right?"

"I agree. I'll see if I can ring her back, if she picks up."

"I wouldn't bother. If we set off now, we should arrive there around the same time."

Katy parked next to Carol's car and switched off the engine. "Now all we have to do is find her. Did she mention if she was going to head for the same spot as yesterday?"

"No, she didn't say. I'm presuming that's the case because all the clues we were after highlighted the area perfectly. There's only one way to find out."

"Okay, before we set off, I think we should arm ourselves, just in case Smalling turns up unexpectedly."

Lorne grinned. "I dread to think what kind of weapons you have lurking in your boot."

Katy removed a length of rope and an iron bar used for changing tyres on a vehicle. "These will do nicely. A bang on the head with this one while you tie him up."

Lorne laughed, then they marched through the entrance to the forest, aware of every crunch and snap the undergrowth made under their feet. Before long, they reached the spot where the teams had searched the previous day. Carol was nowhere to be seen.

"Maybe she's gone farther in." Looking ahead, Lorne pointed at two possible paths. "Eeny meeny… should I call out to her?"

Katy scanned the area around them. "It can't hurt."

"Carol. Where are you, Carol?"

Straining an ear, Katy held up a finger. "Did you hear that? It sounded like it came from over there."

"Let's take this pathway and call out again in a minute or two." Lorne walked ahead of Katy, upping her speed as she got closer to the path. She noticed yet another stone bridge like the one they'd discovered on their previous visit. "Looks promising. Carol? Can you hear me?"

A muffled cry echoed through the trees. "Here, Lorne."

She picked up the sound of distress in the woman's tone, or was that just her mind playing havoc? She shuddered at the thought of being surrounded by the wandering lost souls who lingered there, waiting to be set free. They continued on the path, and Lorne spotted the outline of a figure in a clear patch up ahead.

"Is that her?" Katy asked, peering through the trees.

"It looks like her." Lorne called out, "Carol, is that you?"

"Yes, Lorne. We're here."

"Crap, did she say *we*?"

Lorne sniggered. "Hold on, looks like we're in for another torrid time in the company of Noelle's spirit."

"Great. Let's get this over with."

Lorne and Katy quickly proceeded to the clearing where Carol was standing. A tiny light flickered just in front of her friend.

"Carol, has Noelle remembered anything else?"

"I'm so glad you decided to join us. Yes, Noelle said that her necklace was removed from her neck. It was a family heirloom handed down to her after the demise of her grandmother. Plus, her ring was also stolen. It's engraved, congratulating her on her confirmation when she was thirteen. If Smalling is in possession of those items, it will help you to convict him, won't it?"

As soon as Carol mentioned Smalling's name, a soft groan came from the direction of the light.

"Noelle, if he has your jewellery, it will only work in our favour. Why are you in this part of the forest, Carol?"

"We're still trying to figure that out. Noelle, in which direction should we go now? Guide us, please?" Carol's voice was light and encouraging when she addressed the spirit. The glimmer flickered, becoming brighter, then drifted towards another pathway. "Come on, ladies. She wants us to follow her."

Katy and Lorne glanced at each other. Katy raised her eyebrows and impatiently tapped her watch.

"Come now, Katy. You can spare us an hour of your valuable time, I'm sure," Carol said over her shoulder.

Reluctantly, Katy agreed, and the three women and the spirit continued on their journey. Not long after, Carol halted at the edge of the forest.

Lorne caught up with her. "What is it, Carol?"

"I'm not sure how significant this is. All I can tell you is that Noelle is refusing to let me move any farther along the route."

They had stopped before a roped-off area and a swaying sign reading: DO NOT TRESPASS.

"That's strange. What can it mean? Shall we check it out?" Lorne asked Katy.

"If it says no trespassing, then we've got to abide by that. There's no telling if the property owners have laid any kind of traps in the undergrowth, is there? I wonder if we can get to what lies beyond if we continue around the edge of the forest."

"It's worth a try. Hang on... look." Lorne pointed in the distance beyond the rope.

Carol gasped. "It's a house!"

"Right, here's what I think we should do—get our bearings and try to find the road which leads up to the house. Damn, I never thought to bring a compass with me," Katy said.

"What about our phones? Won't they give us our location?"

Katy withdrew her mobile from her jacket pocket and tutted. "No signal. I should have realised we'd be cut off this far into the forest."

"Okay, then we'll have to do as you suggested. We'll scout the area on the other side of the forest to find the road. It shouldn't be that difficult, should it?"

Carol closed her eyes and made a humming sound. Then she clicked her fingers. "Thomas or Thomsett. That's what I'm picking up from this area, whether it's the name of the road you're after or not, I have no idea."

"That's a start. Thanks, Carol. We should head back to the cars, unless Noelle can give us anything else?"

"No, I don't think so. Coming back here and confronting her pain has drained all her energy. That's why she hasn't formed like she did yesterday. She's determined to offer her guidance in finding the house, if that's okay?"

Katy nodded. "Perfect."

The trek back through the forest took them nearly fifteen minutes. "You should leave your car here and come with us, Carol," Lorne suggested, standing in between both vehicles.

"Hop in, everyone," Katy said. "That makes perfect sense to me."

Katy turned the car while Lorne played around with the sat nav, trying out the names Carol had provided, hoping for a match nearby.

"Bingo! Here we are. Thomsett Way. Take the first left and keep turning left until I say otherwise. Well done, Carol. You've done it again."

"Try and restrain your enthusiasm for now, Lorne. We haven't located the house yet," Katy admonished playfully.

However, Lorne had a good feeling about the information Carol had supplied them with. Carol sat in the back of the car, humming. She didn't speak until Katy pulled up outside a large Victorian house. "This is it!" she cried out in excitement.

"Are you sure, Carol?" Lorne asked, her insides churning.

"Yes, yes! Go! We need to get in there, now."

"Carol, we need you to stay in the car. Do you understand?" Katy instructed. "We need to take things slowly and follow procedure from here. We can't go in there, screaming and shouting at the homeowners."

"I understand. Noelle and I will sit tight and hand the reins over to you two detectives to complete the task. Yes, this is definitely the place." Carol nodded, staring at the house through narrowed eyes.

Lorne and Katy got out of the car and approached the front gate. "How are we going to play this, Katy?"

"Let's see what presents itself and go from there. I'll do all the talking, okay?" Katy warned with a pointed finger.

"Deal."

Katy cleared her throat and rang the doorbell.

A lady in her late fifties opened the door in a very offhand manner. "Yes!"

"We're sorry to trouble you on a cold and dreary morning. We're looking for a family who used to live in this area. I saw your light on and thought I'd stop by and see if you knew them."

"I'll try to help, although I tend not to mix with too many people in the area. What's the name of these people?"

Katy smiled at the woman. "You're very kind. It's Smalling. Do you know them at all?"

The woman frowned and looked Katy and Lorne up and down. "Who wants to know?"

Katy and Lorne produced their warrant cards and thrust them in front of the woman's face. "DI Katy Foster and DS Lorne Warner. Are you Mrs. Smalling?" Katy said.

"No."

Lorne and Katy glanced at each other and grimaced.

"Do you know the Smalling family at all? Are you friends perhaps?" Katy pressed.

"No," the woman stated abruptly a second time.

Katy sighed. "Then I think we've made a mistake. I apologise for inconveniencing you."

Before the woman could shut the door, Lorne asked, "Does your property back onto the forest, Mrs...?"

The woman paused for an instant then said, "Jackman. Yes, it does."

"Would you mind if we took a closer look at the area beyond the Do Not Trespass sign? Did you erect that sign, or has it always been there?"

"My husband erected the sign, and no, you can't. Not without a search warrant. This is private property."

She closed the door before either of them could ask another question. Dejected, they returned to the car, where Carol proceeded to bombard them with questions.

"Was it her? Mrs. Smalling?"

"Nope," Lorne replied.

"No! I don't believe her. Did she say she knew the Smallings?" Carol asked eagerly with an edge of annoyance resonating in her tone.

"No. Look, Carol, I think on this occasion, your abilities have let you down a little. Yes, it's the house we saw from the forest, but as far as being linked to the Smallings, we have no proof of that, yet," Kart said.

"I know there is a major connection here. Will it help if I describe the woman? Bearing in mind that the front door of the house isn't visible to me from where I'm sitting?"

Katy and Lorne twisted in their seats. Without further prompting, Carol reeled off an accurate description of the woman who had answered the door.

"Well, am I right?" Carol asked.

"Spot on," Lorne admitted. "Shit, what do you propose we do now, Katy?"

Katy hit the steering wheel with the heel of her hand then started the engine. "Get a warrant, as the woman suggested. This isn't over yet, ladies, not by a long shot. No one outsmarts us. We'll drop you back to your car, Carol, and head back to the station."

CHAPTER FOURTEEN

Lorne barged through the doors to the incident room, startling the rest of the team.

Katy followed right behind her. "Listen up, everyone. We've got a situation on our hands." Katy walked up to a puzzled-looking Karen and gave her a slip of paper on which she had noted down the address they had just visited. "Run this through the system, Karen. Let me know the proprietor's name and the previous owners' names going back the last five years, will you?"

"Yes, ma'am." Karen immediately hit the keys on her keyboard while Katy informed the rest of the team what had transpired at the forest and at the woman's residence.

"So, let me get this right. You think this woman is Smalling's mother?" AJ asked, sounding confused.

"Yep, that's our assumption. AJ, can you get a warrant for the address, on the grounds that we think she is harbouring a suspect?"

"Umm... not wishing to go against orders, Inspector, but don't you think we should see what Karen comes up with first?"

"You're right, of course. Karen, any luck?"

"Just double-checking another avenue now, boss. Give me two secs... here we are. Okay, I've got a discrepancy to do with the home owners on that address. Yes, the Smallings used to own the property, but then a Mr. Jackman had his name added to the mortgage."

"Was the house sold in between that time?"

"Nope. It never came on the market, and looking at the land registry, the house is still listed in Mrs. Smalling's name."

Lorne gasped. "She's remarried. The snide bitch. She's obviously got something to hide. Otherwise, she would have told us that."

"It seems that way to me. Right, AJ, get that warrant ASAP. Stephen, you and Graham go out to the address and observe the comings and goings. I don't need to tell you to keep yourselves hidden, do I?"

Both men rose from their chairs and put on their jackets.

"No, boss. Discretion will be utmost when we get there," Graham insisted.

Stephen agreed with a brisk nod.

"What do you want me to do, boss?" Lorne asked, eager to have a role in the downfall of the people who'd tried to deceive them.

"Lorne, I want you to get in touch with the relevant teams—forensics and the police dog team—again. I think we'll hit the place heavy-handed, payback for the woman lying to us like that."

"I'll put them on standby for this afternoon."

Lorne placed the calls to the teams then rang Carol to keep her apprised of the situation. After all, the case would have still been in its infancy if Carol hadn't been involved. "Carol, it's me. I don't have long—things are frantic here at the moment."

"What did you find out?"

"That you were right. We think the woman remarried. We're in the process of obtaining a warrant to search the property, as she requested. I'll let you know later what we find out."

"Lorne, you know I wouldn't usually insist tagging along to a scene, but... I think I really should be there when you gain access to the property. I'm sure Noelle will help us find her body."

"I don't know, Carol. You've done enough for us already. Why don't we leave it up to the professionals now to conclude the search and locate the body, eh?"

"What harm can it do, Lorne? The professionals might start digging in the wrong place and get disheartened."

"I can see your logic. Look, it really is Katy's call. Let me ask her and get back to you later, okay?"

"All right. Please consider my request carefully, though. Promise?"

"We will. I promise. I've gotta fly now. Speak later. And, Carol, thanks for your input so far. We couldn't have done this without your help."

"I could do so much more if only you'd agree to let me go to the house with you."

"Nice try. Talk later." Lorne looked up as Katy arrived at her desk. "I just wanted to update Carol. Hope that was okay?"

"Of course. Is she excited?"

"Yes and no. She wants to be there for the search. She thinks Noelle could point the team in the right direction. I'm not a hundred percent sure about that."

"Why not? Are you referring to exposing her and Noelle to the rest of the teams and the possible ridicule attached to that?"

"I suppose so. I told her the choice would be yours in the end."

"Gee, thanks. Well, I vote that she should be there." Lorne's eyes widened. Katy continued, "Don't look at me like that. I know I used to be the biggest sceptic going, but after witnessing Noelle's spirit, it's hard to question the legitimacy of the spirit world. I'm sold on the idea anyway."

"Wow, I never thought I'd hear that come out of your mouth. As soon as we get an action plan together, I'll tell her to meet us at the location."

"You do that. If anyone has a right to be there, it should be Carol, along with Noelle's spirit."

* * *

The convoy of vehicles turned up at Mrs. Jackman's house at four o'clock on the dot. Carol hopped out of the car and walked confidently up the path to the house beside Lorne and Katy. Ringing the doorbell, Katy winked at her two companions.

The door opened, and Mrs. Jackman glared at them with utter contempt. "I told you this morning—no one comes in this house without a warrant."

Katy pushed open the door and handed the warrant paper to the woman. "Excellent. Then you're not disappointed. This gives us the right to search the grounds and your house. Now we can do this in two ways: obstruct us, and we slap the cuffs on you; step aside and let us carry out our work properly, and you will be free to observe our activities. What's it to be, Mrs. Smalling?"

The woman's mouth gaped open for a while, then she recovered her voice. "I've already told you, my name is Jackman."

"It might be at present, however, we have reason to believe you have recently remarried. There's really no use in you trying to hide the truth any longer."

Her shoulders slumped, and they heard movement upstairs. Lorne was the first to react. She whistled for Stephen and Graham and beckoned them to join her. Katy warned Mrs. Jackman to be quiet while Lorne, Stephen, and Graham quietly climbed the stairs. Lorne burst through a door to a back bedroom, to find the same young man she had spotted driving away from the forest the previous day.

He launched at the open window, but Stephen and Graham rugby-tackled him to the floor.

"Get the fuck off me, you jerks."

"Danny Smalling, unless you want resisting arrest added to your charge sheet, I'd advise you to keep calm."

"I ain't Danny Smalling. Don't know what the effing hell you're talking about, lady."

"Stephen, can you search his pockets for ID please?" Lorne noticed the distinctive tattoo on Smalling's forearm. It dawned on her then, that without a doubt, they'd just captured the right man.

The two detectives slapped a pair of cuffs on Smalling's wrists and Stephen withdrew the man's wallet from his trousers. He took out a driving licence and a credit card to confirm his ID.

"Just as I thought. Both you and your mother find it impossible to tell the truth. Take him back to the station, gentlemen, and throw him in a cell. Hit him with a resisting arrest charge for now. We'll add to it once we've searched this place. I'm pretty confident about that."

Smalling sneered and spat in Lorne's face as he was frogmarched towards the door. "You won't find anything here to incriminate me. I've done nothing wrong."

Lorne held on to the vomit dying to escape and wiped the man's spittle from her face with her sleeve. "That's strange. Noelle's spirit tells us otherwise."

Smalling's shocked expression amused Lorne as she watched the intense colour that had filled his cheeks moments before drain away.

The detectives ushered him from the room without giving him the chance to respond, and the four of them descended the stairs under the watchful gaze of Carol, Katy, and Mrs. Jackman.

Carol stepped forward, and before anyone could stop her, she smacked Smalling around the face.

"What the f—," Smalling started to object.

Carol cut him off mid-sentence. "That's from Noelle, you despicable excuse of a human being. How dare you take the life of an innocent young woman like that?"

"You're insane, woman. I ain't hurt nobody. Tell 'em, Ma!"

His mother shook her head, as if recognising how pointless it was to keep defending her son.

"Get him out of my sight," Katy demanded.

Carol left the hallway, and Lorne followed her into the lounge, where she walked up to the French doors and looked out at the garden. "She's out there. Two people in this house know where

Noelle's body is buried—Danny and his mother, not that she will admit it."

"Shall I try and force it out of her? Make some threats?" Lorne asked, willing to do what was necessary to get to the truth.

Carol shook her head. "It's not going to help, Lorne. Let me try and summon Noelle up. Now that Danny's out of the way, she might come forward."

"Do you want to take a wander outside? Will that help?"

"Yep, I was thinking the same. Leave me to it for a few minutes." Carol pulled open the door.

"Call me if I can assist at all. The light will be fading soon." Lorne looked up at the sky.

Carol stepped onto the patio. She held out her arms and raised her head heavenwards, silently beckoning Noelle's spirit to show up.

Lorne went back into the hallway and pulled Katy to one side. "Can we give Carol a few minutes before we let the teams get down to business?"

"Ten minutes is all we can spare, Lorne. Time is getting on."

Lorne and Katy asked the teams to be patient then went into the lounge to watch Carol.

"There!" Lorne pointed at the dull light that had emerged close to Carol's side. The hairs on her neck reacted, and she glanced at Katy, who had tears in her eyes. They clutched hands then punched the air.

"This is it, Lorne."

They observed, their fingers tightly crossed, as Carol walked around the garden. She finally came to a halt close to a wooden shed in the corner. Carol looked back up at the house and pointed at the spot.

"She's done it," Lorne cried joyfully.

"Don't get too excited just yet. We've been here before, remember? I'll instruct the team to begin digging there."

The cadaver dog indicated that they had hit the jackpot, and within an hour, the forensics team discovered Noelle's body buried four feet beneath the surface.

Mixed emotions circulated Lorne's body as the events unfolded. "He couldn't even be bothered to bury her at the correct depth. Bastard," she muttered under her breath.

Carol placed an arm around Lorne's shoulder and whispered, "She'll have the burial she deserves soon enough, in the presence of her friends and family."

EPILOGUE

Everyone was jubilant when Lorne and Katy returned to the station and shared the news. Lorne listened while Katy rang the Chesterfields and informed them of their daughter's death. She found it a surreal moment when Katy ran through the events leading up to the discovery of their daughter's body.

Lorne smiled at the tears welling up in Katy's eyes as Mrs. Chesterfield grudgingly accepted that Noelle would never walk through her front door again then thanked Katy for bringing their daughter back home.

A thorough search of Mrs. Jackman's house resulted in the evidence the team needed to throw the book at her and her son. Sitting in Mrs. Jackman's jewellery box was Noelle's ring and the heirloom necklace Carol had mentioned that morning in the forest.

Relieved they had solved the case in record time, Katy ordered the team to join her at the pub after work. Sean Roberts surprised them all when he walked into the lounge bar and announced that he would be staying with the team after all.

Lorne took him aside. "So it was actually on the cards then? You leaving, I mean?"

He nodded. "It certainly was, right up until this afternoon, Lorne."

"Oh, what changed your mind, Sean?"

"You guys. Look around us—this team is remarkable. How many other teams could honestly solve a cold case within a week? You didn't exactly have a mountain of clues to chase up."

"No. But we did have divine intervention, I suppose you'd call it. There's no way we would have solved this case without Noelle's spirit prompting and showing us the way."

"Hmm… I'm afraid the jury is still out for me on that front, Lorne."

"Well, the truth is always out there, as they say. It's just a matter of digging it up, no pun intended. I'm glad you're staying anyway. I don't think Katy could have stood getting used to another chief inspector this early on in her career. Between you and me, how do you think she's doing?"

He sighed and glanced over at Katy. "She'll never be you, Lorne. That's for sure. Let me put it this way—she's an adequate substitute."

"We make an excellent team. You're right about that. Right, if you'll excuse me, I have a family to get home to. I'm glad you're staying, Sean. Better the devil you know, and all that."

"Cheeky. See you in the morning."

Lorne said her farewells to the rest of the team then drove home in the dark, her fingers tapping merrily to the sounds of Luther Vandross booming out of the car stereo.

She opened the back door to find Tony and Charlie looking upset. Her mood dipped instantly. "What's wrong? Is it one of the dogs?"

"Henry hasn't been too good today, Mum."

Lorne threw her bag on the floor and knelt by the back door. She peered under the kitchen table. Her old pal, who was lying on a rug, raised his head to look at her. His eyes had lost their usual sparkle.

"Come on, boy. Come and give your Mum a cuddle."

Henry struggled to get to his feet then crossed the floor, swaying from side to side. She held out her arms, and his tail managed the faintest of wags. He licked her face and sat down beside her. Lorne cuddled the dog and whispered, "I love you, boy."

Henry settled down and placed his head on her lap. A few moments later, his body shuddered and he took his final breath.

Heartbroken, Charlie ran into her mother's arms. They both sobbed openly whilst stroking their treasured friend. Lorne glanced at Tony; even the hardened ex-agent was wiping tears from his eyes.

Lorne knew she had to hold things together for her daughter's sake. Swallowing the lump constricting her throat, she placed a finger under Charlie's chin and lifted her head to look at her. "He's in a better, pain-free place now, darling. We'll never forget him, and he'll always be around us."

Lorne ran her hand over her beloved dog's head and down the length of his neck. Resting her palm over his silent heart, she whispered, "Farewell, my devoted friend. Farewell."

Note to the reader.

Thank you for reading Rough Justice; I sincerely hope you enjoyed reading this novella as much as I loved writing it.

If you liked it, please consider posting a short review as genuine feedback is what makes all the lonely hours writers spend producing their work worthwhile.

14819157R00094

Printed in Great Britain
by Amazon.co.uk, Ltd.,
Marston Gate.